THE JERSEY DEVIL

A COLLECTION OF UTTER SPECULATION

THE JERSEY DEVIL

Melissa D. Sullivan

LCW Allingham

H. A. Callum

River Eno

Susan Tulio

A COLLECTION OF UTTER SPECULATION

ISBN: 978-1-946702-34-0

Cover design by Adam C. Allingham

Published by Freeze Time Media

In memory of Dan Kinter

Thank you for making us laugh while you were making sure we were properly punctuated and grammatically correct. You are truly missed.

Acknowledgments

The Writers Block would again like to voice our appreciation to Patricia Allingham Carlson for generously allowing us the use of her artwork. Always beautiful. Always impressive. We thank you! We would also like to give a huge thanks to Adam C. Allingham for the outstanding book cover design. You nailed it again! And as always a big shout out to our editor and publisher Di Freeze of Freeze Time Media. Thank you Di, for being fast, efficient, and always ready to hash it out with us when we disagree with your edits. You're the best!

And perhaps most importantly, (or last but not least, whatever) big hugs and many thank you's to our friends and families for their unending support. And to the readers of "The Lost Colony of Roanoke: A Collection of Utter Speculation." It is because of you that we are back with more tales of speculation.

Acknowledgments

Contents

Foreword

Folklore is defined as popular myths and beliefs relating to a particular place and circulated orally among a people. The folktale of the Jersey Devil began in 1735. As legend has it, the 13th child of a family, local to the New Jersey Pine Barrens, was born cursed and deformed. The elusive creature moves quickly through the Barrens and is said to resemble a Wyvern with a horse or dragon head, leathery wings, and have horns and cloven hooves. The Writers Block writers have tried to capture the spirit of the folklore tradition by creating their own tales of wonder and speculation. Enjoy!

Land of Hope and Dreams

Melissa D. Sullivan

Sidonie scraped her fingernail against the bio lab's reinforced Plexiglas window and scowled at the rain that was falling for the third freakin' day in a row.

It wasn't fair. Her mothers always went out, no matter whether it was raining or if the acidity level in the sandy Pine Barrens' soil was elevated. Just because Sid made one stupid mistake didn't mean she didn't know how to properly secure her biohazard coverall. Besides, she knew that if she asked nicely, Mom would let her go.

But, as ever and always and until the end of known space and time, it was Maman that was the problem.

It wasn't like Sid had meant to leave a petri dish open. And it certainly wasn't as if Sid's mistake had done anything near as bad as "possibly setting the whole mission back months" or "putting their entire project at risk," as Maman had ranted at dinner.

"If you can't take your responsibilities seriously, I don't know how you're ever going to be an asset to this or any other study team."

And Maman said Sid was the drama queen.

As usual, Mom had stepped in and tried to make peace.

"We are living in too tight quarters to have blood feuds," she had said, touching Sid on her shoulder and smiling winningly at her wife. "And I've grown attached to our little family. So, please, for my sake, cut it out before I donate both of you to science."

"Fine," Maman grunted into her tofu.

"Fine," Sid grumbled into her water glass.

Then, Maman pointed to Sid across the narrow kitchenette table with her chopstick. "As long as she admits that she's got a lot to prove before she can be trusted again."

That, of course, gave Sid no choice other than to storm from the table into her pod and blast electronicore for the rest of the night. She hadn't spoken to Maman since then.

It was so unfair, Sid thought, scraping harder at the window, frowning at her reflection that in the watery glass looked disturbingly like Maman: tawny skin stretched over a high forehead, wideset cedar-colored eyes and a cloud of black-brown curls. Of course she knew how important their work was. Mom and Maman had only six months to catalogue all the flora and fauna of the Pine Barrens before the U.S. government brought their equipment to drill one of the last clean water sources on the Eastern Seaboard. And Sid, who had been traveling with her mothers since she was born, was practically an eco-botanist herself. If she was allowed to help like she was perfectly capable of, maybe they would be able to find something—anything—of enough scientific importance that would convince the politicos to hold off.

Instead, Maman took one dumb slipup and wrote off Sid as a lost cause.

Sid breathed out hard, fogging the window, and drew a frowny face. From one of the eyes, she traced a trickle of tears and then, blinking hard, put her forehead on the cool glass and looked out at the rain.

An eye stared back at her.

Sid jerked back sharply and then wiped away the rest of the condensation. There—only a few centimeters away—was the oddest animal she had ever seen.

No more than half a meter high, the creature was dark brown and scaly, with a long, narrow snout. It was standing on the edge of the lab's sill, its head cocked to one side, staring at Sid out of one amber eye. It was crouched low on its hind legs but when Sid moved toward the window for a closer look, it stood up, its small front arms curled under its chest.

Sid was afraid to move, wishing her handheld wasn't across the room. She had never seen anything like it. Was it a lizard? Some sort of diseased bird? It did look rather scrawny, with delicate ribs showing under the lighter skin of its chest. It had the walleyes of prey but the small arms it kept close to its chest looked like they ended in three wicked claws. And was that a spike on the end of its long tail?

She really needed to get a picture, if she was going to be able to categorize it decisively.

Maybe, she thought with a jump of excitement, maybe it was something entirely new. Something no other scientist had ever seen before. Something Sid could use to show Maman that she wasn't a complete screwup.

But first, she would need proof. Empirical evidence, as Maman said.

She had to get to her handheld.

Moving as little as possible, Sid slowly stood. Maybe, if she was careful enough...

The creature stretched its neck up and took a step back, as if getting ready to leap.

"No, little guy," Sid said softly. "It's okay. I just want to take a quick pic. Don't you want to be famous?"

The creature cocked its head to the side, as if considering the possibility of becoming a reptile celebrity.

Then it promptly bounded off into the driving rain.

"Merde," Sid muttered and briefly considered going after it. But it would take her almost five minutes to get all the necessary protective gear on, not to mention the explanations about why she was going out into a semi-toxic environment in the rain and right before dinner.

"Siddie!" Mom called from the dining unit. "Food!"

Sid grunted in frustration. Proving her Maman wrong would have to wait.

Sid poked at her croque madame, the savory smell of real cheese and butter making her stomach twist. It was her favorite and Maman's, too. Another peace offering, to get them in better moods, Sid would bet. But Sid wasn't the one in a bad mood.

"Any luck?" Mom asked Maman, as she set two glasses of white burgundy on the table.

Maman took a glass and shot half of it down in one gulp. Her blue-black braids were twisted in a particularly messy bun high on her head, and her sable face looked sallow and drawn.

"Nothing, cheri. I was on the vidphone all morning, but it looks like there's nothing to be done."

Mom set the pan down on the anti-mag stove and pulled off her oven mitts, her freckled face flushed with heat or scientific indignation.

"But what about our discovery? Surely a new species of fern is worthy of conservation. Or at least a couple of months before the whole Pine Barren becomes an industrial site?"

Maman pounded her first on the table once, then again. "It doesn't matter. All they see is an environment that's already been ruined by climate change, pollutants and invasive species. They don't even care about our damnable research. They just want to get what they can before there's nothing left. Goddamn it!"

"I'm so sorry, hun," Mom said.

"I wish there was some way to get through to them. To show them that there is some worth in trying to save this place, even if we made missteps in the past.

But they are so set on their 'priorities' that nothing and no one can change their minds."

Maman covered her eyes with one hand and sniffed quietly.

Sid's mouth fell open in shock. Though Mom was a softy, tearing up at every commercial on the vid, Sid had never seen Maman cry, not once. Not even when Sid accidentally contaminated a whole series of rare Psilocybe Galindoi spore specimens with Laffy Taffy when she was two.

Mom reached out for Maman's hand and clasped it. "It's not what we wanted," she said. "But we've gotten a lot done. How long do we have left?"

Maman wiped her eyes and shook her head. "I don't know. A week. At most a month."

Sid stabbed her croque madame, causing the yellow yolk to run down the side of the bread and pool on the plate. What a bunch of merde. All their work, trying to preserve one of the most unique ecosystems in North America, rendered worthless in five seconds.

No, Sid decided. Something had to be done.

"Mom," Sid said carefully. "What if you did find something? Like a new species of animal or something? Do you think people would care then?"

"Come on, Sid. Use that brain of yours," Maman said. "What are the chances of us finding any new, significant mammals?"

"Well, maybe not a mammal," Sid said, feeling a little smug. "But maybe a lizard."

Maman sighed. "Despite some of our early hopes, there are no reptiles indigenous to the Pine Barrens that can't be found elsewhere. Which you would have known if you actually did any of the report summaries on time, like you said you would."

Sid was about to open her mouth and tell her mother exactly how wrong she was.

And then she closed it. Wouldn't it be more satisfying if she could find it herself? Surprise Maman and Mom and save the study and prove once and for all that she was a responsible and brilliant scientist? And, more importantly, that Maman was completely, utterly and astoundingly wrong?

Sid pictured the look on Maman's face when Sid presented her with the exact thing that would save them all. She felt a smile crease her lips for the first time in days.

Yes, that was exactly what she needed to do.

"What is it, Sid?" Mom asked. "What are you thinking about?"

"Nothing," she said, shrugging. "Just thinking about something I saw today. Can I take my dinner in my pod? I've got a paper due for my online biochem class."

"Sure, hun," Mom said.

Sid stood up and hurried to her room. She had a lot to get ready before the morning.

As soon as the sky turned pink, Sid crept out of her pod, already wearing the spare, low tech hazmat suit, which unlike her mothers' suits didn't have any of the built-in recording equipment but did offer semi-adequate protection from the acid rain. No matter. She would use the old 3-D camcorder and, in a pinch, her handheld. The camcorder was bulky and not waterproof, so Sid had packed it away in her carryall which she would have to carry on her back. Her handheld went in one of her hazmat suit's front pockets, making it easily accessible for a quick pic. She'd stayed up most of the night, programing it so that she only needed to tap it for recording: once for a pic, twice for video.

This time, if she could find the creature, she wasn't taking any chances.

The hardest part was going to be getting outside without waking her mothers in their pod on the other side of the lab. Even though the whole area was going to be cleared and leveled so they could get the heavy drilling equipment in, as part of the study, her mothers had to promise the Franco-American Alliance that their "home environment" was adequately sealed to limit any potential cross-contamination. The airlocks, though the latest of Franco-American technology, were somewhat noisy. Luckily, her mothers' door was closed and Sid was able to cross the main room of the pod without falling over her massive boots.

Reaching the main exit of the lab, Sid pushed the button to release the inner door seal. A whoosh of air rushed out and then the heavy metal door popped open. Sid paused for a moment, listening for any movement, then slipped into the pressurized chamber and pulled the door behind her, wincing when it clanged. Quickly, she pushed the exit button, to pressurize the inner door and release the outer door. Sid knew the whole process took fifteen seconds but it felt like an eternity, standing there while the chamber filled with air from the outside.

"Come on, come on, come on," she whispered.

Finally, the pressure indicator switched from red to green. Sid pushed open the outer door and stepped out into the wetlands of the Pine Barrens.

It was cooler outside but humid, with the rain not so much falling from the sky but hanging around her in the air like mist.

Sid pulled out her handheld, raised her visor and tapped two times, aiming the camera at her head.

"Sidonie Dubois-Jones. Project Artemis. Date: 9 September 2063. Time: approximately oh-six-hundred. I am beginning my search for the... specimen, which, at last sighting, went due west."

Sid tapped the handheld again and started to walk toward the stand of trees where the little lizard had disappeared. The squishy ground ran with rivulets of water. Her boots stepped on a root, and Sid almost went down.

Merde. This was going to be tough going. But she had to find the creature.

"How's your head?" Lucy asked her wife, glancing up from her tablet as Heloise finally decided to brave the light of day.

"Fine," Heloise grumbled, wincing as thunder cracked outside, her head already pounding from the constant patter of the rain against the lab's roof. She was so stupid. Staying up all night and finishing a whole bottle of wine alone wasn't going to fix anything.

After pouring herself coffee and loading it with saccharine and cream, she gingerly sat next to her wife. The clacking of the keys felt like nails between her eyes.

"Can you not type so loud?"

Lucy snorted but paused. "Poor thing. Did you sleep at all?"

"Not really," Heloise said, rubbing her sandy eyes. "All I could do was think about everything we've worked on for the last year, poof, up in smoke. What do you think about Senator Booker?"

"Didn't you try her office last time?"

"Yes, but this time she's running for president," Heloise said. "Maybe this could be a national story. Part of her platform about reversing climate change."

Lucy's mouth twisted. "Really?"

Heloise sighed. "I know, I know. But I need to do something, no matter how pointless it will be in the end."

Lucy murmured something supportive and resumed typing.

Heloise sighed again and took a sip of her coffee. Her wife had the right idea. Even if they had to leave, they still had a little bit of time and as scientists they had an obligation to preserve what they could before the drills came. Really, she should stop pitching at windmills and get back to work, wrapping up her projects in a way that would allow her to finish them after they returned to their labs at the université.

But she wasn't ready to give up. Not yet.

And then there was Sid. Heloise groaned. She hadn't meant to be that harsh, but ever since Sid had turned fourteen, her daughter had mutated into some kind of hormone-driven surly stranger. Like this recent dustup. All Heloise was trying to say was that if Sid wasn't diligent about fulfilling her daily responsibilities, like cleaning the traps in the fish tank or checking that all of the experiments were secure for the night before she left the lab, she would never learn the tenacity necessary to be an eco-biologist, which was exactly what Sid said she wanted. Of course, Sid had started taking such umbrage to Heloise's gentle reminders that she had stopped communicating with her almost completely, directing all of the parent-related conversation to Lucy, who was often too soft on their daughter.

It had been so much easier, when Sid was small and would follow Heloise around the lab, chirping questions in her little girl voice and running her own "experiments," mixing blue and red dye in test tubes. That was the part Heloise missed the most about Sid's transformation into a teenager: talking to her daughter.

"Did you talk to Sid this morning?" Heloise asked, trying to sip her coffee casually.

"Not yet. Still sleeping. She was up late, too."

"Why? For school? Does she need help on something?"

"You could ask her, you know," Lucy said, giving her a pointed look over her screen.

"No," Heloise said, briskly. "I'm sure it's fine."

Lucy murmured again, though this murmur didn't sound supportive.

"Pardon?"

"Oh, nothing," Lucy said, rolling her eyes. "Just musing about inherited traits."

"Well," Heloise said, setting her mug down and pushing herself up from the kitchen table. "It's almost ten. Sid should be getting ready to log in, if she isn't already late."

Sid's pod door was still shut. Heloise tapped lightly on the metal.

"Sid? Can I come in?"

There was no answer, so Heloise pushed the door gently open.

"Sid? Are you still sleeping?"

The room was dim and messy, with the windows still darkened and clothes strewn across the floor and the bed.

The bed was empty. A sudden rush of pure panic killed all remnants of her hangover. Heloise turned on her heel and strode over to the computer array next to the kitchenette, quickly calling up the lab's surveillance files. Lucy looked up from her work and, reading the alarm on her wife's face, stood.

"What is it?"

Heloise pulled up the video for the main cabin and started running it from last night's dinner, triple time.

"Sid's not in her room," Heloise said. "Did you check the lab?"

"I got my tablet from there. Do you think—?"

"She ran away? No. I don't think so." Heloise looked out the side window, the rain still coming down in sheets. Nom de Dieu, what fool-headed scheme had that girl cooked up now?

Sid was getting a little pissed. So far, there was no sign of the creature. Only endless new growth that made walking difficult in the rain, which had been falling in earnest for the last hour. Water was leaching into the neck of her gear, which was obviously not as airtight as the manufacturer advertised. Though the pH wasn't enough to be corrosive, that meant she was probably breathing in more sulfur dioxide then was good for her. She really had to be quick.

She looked around. She was in one of the older tree groves, consisting of thick pitch pines that had struggled on for years in the normally hot, dry summers, their roots needing to go down deep into the sandy soil for water. Now, with the newly tropical conditions on the Eastern Seaboard, moss clung up their sides and new ferns sprouted around their bases. They looked to be one of the species her mom had already classified, but she might as well take a closer look, just in case. Sid leaned down and reached into her pocket to get her handheld.

Suddenly, there was a flash of brown in front of her visor.

Sid stepped back in surprise and fell backwards hard on her butt.

There it was. The creature, standing at its full one-meter height, a piece of new fern curling out of its beak. It looked back at Sid with a look of slight annoyance.

"Oh, hey, little dude," Sid said. "I've been looking for you everywhere. Is that breakfast?"

The creature lifted its chin and took another slow chomp.

Perfect, Sid thought. Now, if she could get a picture or better yet, a video. But her carryall was slung around her right shoulder and, sitting on the ground, she couldn't get to her handheld, which was deep in her side pocket.

Sid started to shift, trying to get onto her knees.

The creature didn't like that. It dropped the fern and stood up on its hind legs, straight as it could, puffed out its chest and unfurled a ruff of thinly ribbed skin, like a frilled-necked lizard. It hissed at Sid, and Sid, not sure if this was a real or fake threat display, froze.

Then it promptly turned around and fled back into the forest.

"Damn it!" Sid said. She scrambled up off the wet ground and started running after the creature. There was no way she was going to lose this chance again.

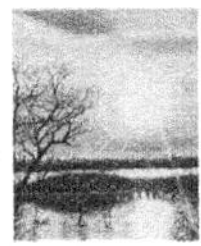

"Luce!" Heloise called. "I found her!"

"When? Where?" Lucy stumbled over from her screen, where she had been reviewing footage of the side exits.

Heloise tapped her screen, zooming in on a grainy shot of the main airlock. "She left this morning. Around dawn."

Lucy frowned. "What on earth is she thinking? I told her that the pH levels were going to be borderline all this week. And we just got her asthma under control from the fall pollen."

Heloise squinted at the screen, trying to get details from the black and white image. The camera aimed at the main entrance wasn't one of their best, as it was only used for security purposes, and who the hell was going to break into a scientific lab in the middle of the Pine Barrens?

"Well, she seems to have gear, but nothing for an overnight. Maybe something for school?"

Lucy shook her head. "She didn't mention anything. Can you track her?"

"Not well." Heloise minimized the security cam's video and pulled up a topographical map of the area, which showed a little green dot moving in halting jumps toward the west. "See? There's something interfering with her handheld's signal. I can track her to a radius about 100 meters but that's about it."

"Can you call her?"

"I tried. But she's not picking up."

Lucy moved the screen down slightly. "She seems to be headed to Leeds Ravine. With all this rain, isn't there a possibility of a flash flood?"

"Highly unlikely," Heloise said, but suddenly she wasn't sure. What if there was a flash flood and Sid somehow slipped down the ravine and got swept away? It was remote, but it could happen. And because Sid's common sense seemed to have taken a permanent holiday, she would probably go right to where there was the most danger out of some sort of adolescent self-destructive instinct.

"But to be safe, I'll go out after her," Heloise said, pushing back from the computer.

Lucy gathered the hazmat helmet and boots while Heloise pull the heavy plastic coveralls over her pajamas. What the hell was Sid thinking? When Heloise got ahold of her, they were going to have a long chat about protocols and professionalism and what could have happened to her if she had fallen and broken a leg or got swept away by a flash flood of chemical-soaked runoff. Not to mention that Sid was going to be subject to one of the world's first transnational groundings.

"Please, dear," her wife said, handing her the helmet and zipping up the front of her suit. "When you find her, try your best not to kill her. She is your only daughter."

"Don't worry," Heloise growled. "She's not getting off that easy."

Sid was going as fast as she could, but the ground was boggy and she kept losing the creature in the foliage. A couple of times, the creature stopped, intrigued by a bit of greenery, and Sid had started to reach into her pocket, but before she could get a clear shot, the creature darted off again. She'd been traveling for almost an hour and the gear was starting to weigh on her. Also, the SO2 indicator on her hazmat's wrist was beginning to show elevated levels. She really couldn't stay out much longer.

The creature disappeared over what appeared to be a small ridge that Sid couldn't see over.

"Merde and branleur."

Sid rushed up the ridge and found herself teetering at the top of a steep muddy slope that led down to a rocky creek bed. Unable to stop her momentum, she lost her footing on a pile of wet leaves and slid toward the creek. She ditched her carryall and with both hands desperately tried to grab hold of one of the spindly bushes around her, but she was going too fast and the slope was too slippery. Waving her arms wildly but uselessly, she slid all the way down the hill, hitting every sharp rock, until she landed with a splash on the edge of the creek.

"Fan-fucking-tastic," Sid muttered, lying flat on her back, feeling like she had been rolled around in a rock tumbler. She tried to push herself up, but a wrenching pain in her shoulder made her gasp and fall back into the soft mud.

Well, this had been an unmitigated disaster, Sid thought as she started slowly sinking into the ground. Maybe she would stay here and archeologists a thousand years from now would find her and wonder what strange people buried their dead in yellow plastic.

The sky flashed above her and the clouds opened up, the rain covering Sid's visor in fat drops. Now, there would be no visibility and no actual sense in continuing. Sid sighed and tried again to push herself up from the mud with her one good arm.

There, on the opposite bank, not three meters from where Sid was lying, was the damned creature. It was so close, she could see what looked like a third eyelid blinking rapidly across its yellow iris. It was standing pretty much in one spot, but making odd jerking movements.

Maybe it's stuck, Sid thought. Her heart started to pound with excitement. This was it. Maybe if she could reach her pocket, without moving any other part of her body, she could get one clear, perfect shot.

As she touched the hard plastic of her handheld, there was another rumble of thunder. Then another, though closer and with more of a vocal quality.

Sid frowned. That didn't sound like any thunder she had ever heard.

There was another roar, and this time, Sid saw a movement in the dark woods on the bank behind the creature. There, stepping out of the dark forest, was the most terrifying thing Sid had ever seen.

Sid lost any thought of scientific detachment.
"Help!" she screamed. "Someone! Help me!"

Heloise pulled out her handheld. From the tracking dot on the tiny screen, Sid was nearly to the ravine. Which was astounding since the entire way was rough country with unstable wetlands. And she'd covered it in less than an hour.

Maybe her daughter was more tenacious then she thought.

Heloise reached the high point before the land sloped down towards the bottom of the ravine and pulled her scopes out. There. Heloise could see the edge of Sid's yellow hazmat down at the bottom of the ravine, about a hundred meters away. She appeared to be lying prone on the edge of the creek somewhat submerged.

Was she looking at something? Gathering samples? She was sure to catch a cold, Heloise thought with a grumble. And then she was going to be so very, very grounded.

Then, a roar like a rocket taking off shook the pines.

Heloise shifted her view over to the source of the sound. Heloise caught the edge of a slithering movement in the dark wetness on the opposite bank. The scopes automatically zoomed in.

There, standing among the pines, was the largest reptile Heloise had ever seen. Standing more then six meters tall and covered in interlocking brown scales, it had a long narrow snout and a great spikey ridge extending from its head. Its small arms ended in three wickedly sharp claws.

And it was lumbering toward her child.

"Help!" Sid screamed. "Someone! Help me!"

Heloise flung herself down the ravine.

Sid heard a crashing sound behind her and twisted her neck around. Maman was careening crazily down the slippery hill. She fell on Sid and yanked on her arms, as if ready to drag her all the way back to the lab.

"Ow!" Sid yelped, as Maman's grip on her arm wrenched her shoulder painfully.

"Get up! Get up! We have to go. Now!"

No, no, no. She wasn't leaving without a picture. Sid flailed, managing to free her one good arm, and fumbled for her handheld in her front pocket.

"Sidonie!" Maman said, still pulling on her other arm. "Come on! Allons-y!"

"Maman, stop! I need to—" Sid finally freed her handheld and tried to line up the pic.

A roar shook the trees again.

"No!" Maman shouted. Letting go of her arm, Maman flung herself in front of Sid, putting her arms out as wide as she could and waving frantically.

“Get back!” Maman yelled, her voice crackling over the helmet’s speaker.

The monster roared again and took a step closer.

Sid tried to grab her mother’s leg.

“No, Maman! Stop!” she shouted. “I think—I think it’s trying to protect its baby!”

Her mother twisted toward her, her eyes crazed behind her visor. “What?”

Sid pointed jerkily to the small reptile, still jerking on the bank. “Look! It’s stuck. If I can ...”

“No, Sid!”

But Sid was already halfway toward the creature.

“It’s okay, it’s okay,” Sid whispered, sliding herself across the rough creek bed. When she was less than a meter away, Sid saw that it had gotten one of its feet trapped under one of the heavy gray rocks lining the water. Carefully—so carefully—Sid reached out and with one slow hand, nudged the rock off the creature’s spiny foot.

As soon as the rock slid a few centimeters to the left, the creature darted off to the bank and underneath the shelter of its mother’s broad belly. The monster craned its enormous head down, checking to see that its baby was safe and then stood up, looking directly at Maman and Sid with cold, calculating eyes. Then, it unfurled enormous wings. Thin membranes shone between strong spines, like a bat. A bolt of lightning lit the sky, and the beast was outlined in terrifying starkness.

“Fascinating,” Sid said, and then reached for her handheld.

"Sid!" yelled Maman.

The monster roared, the sound a physical force against Sid's chest. In its wide-open mouth, a double row of sharp teeth glistened wetly.

"Maman!"

"I'm coming!"

The creature roared again and launched itself toward Sid.

Sid felt her mother's weight fall on top of her, pushing the air out of her lungs. A gust of air rushed over both of them as the creature swooped above them and disappeared into the sky.

Then all was still.

"Ma petite chou-chou," Maman said, her gloves scrabbling at the side of Sid's helmet. "Are you hurt? Please, mon Dieu, say something!"

Sid pushed at her mother's heavy weight, trying to catch her breath. "You're squishing me."

Maman stood and then yanked Sid roughly up. "Come on, let's get the hell out of here."

Lucy wouldn't let Sid go, even after Sid had stopped shaking. Sid was incoherent when Heloise had first dragged her into the lab, so they had had to strip her to make sure she didn't have any broken bones or abrasions. Other than a strained shoulder, there didn't seem to be any serious injuries.

Still, as soon as the soaked suit was off, Sid had started shaking, either from cold or shock, her teeth chattering. Heloise wrapped Sid in blankets hastily warmed in the dryer and carried her lanky body to her and Lucy's double bed. Lucy crawled in beside her and held her tight, murmuring comforting sounds in her ears.

Heloise slumped to the floor, exhausted and completely confused. What had they seen, exactly? It looked... well, it looked like a dinosaur. Sort of. Or a really ugly bird maybe? But with scales? That didn't make sense.

She rubbed her eyes. There had to be some sort of reasonable explanation.

"Hun," Lucy whispered. "Is she sleeping?"

Heloise checked her daughter's face. Amazingly, Sid had fallen asleep, her mouth open.

"Yes," Heloise nodded and then brushed one of Sid's curls off her forehead.

"So, what happened?" Lucy asked.

Heloise shook her head. "I already told you."

"Come on," Lucy said, with her best give-me-a-freakin'-break look. "You can't expect me to believe that you and your daughter went off into the Pine Barrens and almost got eaten by the Jersey Devil and her starving baby? Next, you're going to tell me that the Loch Ness Monster is a really a plesiosaur."

"I know, I know," Heloise groaned, leaning down into her hands. "But there was something there. I mean, I saw it."

"Maman?" Sid said suddenly, her voice alarmed.

"Hey, baby," Heloise said softly. "It's okay. You're home. I'm here."

"No." Sid struggled to free herself from the blankets.

"It's okay, baby," Heloise said again. "You're safe."

"No," Sid said again, freeing one of her arms. "My handheld."

Kids. Even when almost eaten by a mythical creature, they were still worried about their phones. Heloise shared a look with her wife and then went to the other room. Searching through the hastily discarded clothes, she extracted Sid's handheld, which seemed to be soaked through. She went back to the bedroom and handed it to Sid.

"Oh, Sid," Lucy said, when she saw the water dripping off the device. "Don't worry. We'll get you another one."

Sid shook her head and then unlocked the screen. After a couple of flicks, she turned the screen towards Heloise.

"Look," she whispered.

There, on the screen, was the creature—the honest-to-Dieu Jersey Devil—its wings spread out against the silver sky.

Heloise's mouth dropped open.

"I think," Sid croaked, "you owe me an apology."

P Allingham Carlson

Seeking Monsters

LCW Allingham

New Jersey - 1969

The fire jumped from the crudely dug pit and raced beneath the dry bed of pine needles before suddenly flaring up next to Jerry and Dawn. As Jerry pushed Dawn back from the flames and stomped on them, his friends stared blankly at him. They were all more than a little stoned, having come out into the Barrens to celebrate Dawn and Jerry's last week in Jersey with some cold beers and some sweet Mary Jane.

"If it reaches the trees, the whole forest could go up in flames!" Jerry shouted, grabbing beers from the hands of his slack-jawed friends and pouring them on the fire.

"Jer, something's in the woods!" Dawn cried, her wide eyes following the trail of fire to the dark line of pine trees.

Jerry picked up the cooler of ice and dumped it over the path of the fire. He'd grown up in these woods, spent countless peaceful hours beneath the dark pines. He had to stop the blaze.

The fire surged forward and he desperately chased it with beer, stomping wet earth over flares, closer and closer to the tree line when suddenly something pushed him back, onto his ass.

Two eyes, large and luminous, glowered at him in the smokey night. It was a…a deer?

"Jer. Jer, get away from it," Dawn hissed behind him, but Jerry was transfixed as the creature stepped from the shadows of the trees and stomped on the last of the flames, squelching sparks beneath its heavy hooves. It flapped massive leathery wings and a cold gust blew the last of the embers back into the fire pit, where they died. Jerry rose to his feet, his heart pommeling his ribs, seeing only the beaming eyes in the sudden darkness.

"I'm sorry," he said.

The creature hissed and leapt away, another cold wind blasting into Jerry's face as it took to the sky.

Jerry's friends flicked their lighters on, giggling over the near disaster.

"Did you all see that? The Jersey Devil. I swear I saw the Jersey Devil."

"You're so high," came a giggled reply. "If it was the Jersey Devil, we'd all be dead now, man. He, like, eats people and shit."

Jerry stumbled over to Dawn. "I think I should take you home," he said.

"You can't leave the party!" their friends protested.

"The party's over," Jerry said, collecting the empty

beer cans into the cooler. "We almost burned the forest down. You gotta be more careful out here."

"See you later, guys," Dawn said, picking up the last of the cans. She was quiet as they made their way through the forest with only the flicker of Jerry's Bic. When branches cracked in the dark woods around them, Dawn jumped and clung tightly to Jerry's hand.

It wasn't until they were in the car and driving back toward the Garden State Parkway that she spoke.

"You saw that thing," she said. "In the woods."

"I saw it." Jerry kept his eyes on the road. He wasn't as stoned as Dawn but he was rattled. Not by the creature though. "It wasn't — it wasn't bad."

"Jerry, that was the Jersey Devil," she said. "You know my mom's always going on about it. She swears it ate her dad's chickens when she was a kid."

"Yeah, but it's not like anyone has any stories about how it hurt people," Jerry said. "All it did was put out the fire. The fire our dumbass friends started."

"My mom is going to freak out when I tell her," Dawn said, a low chuckle rising in her chest.

"You think she'll be happier about us going to San Fran if she knows the Jersey Devil's after us?" Jerry joked.

"You know she won't. She loves you, but she doesn't understand why we can't get married here."

"Get married here, live here, stay here until we die, where nothing ever changes."

"You got it, baby. Born Jersey, die Jersey. Jersey forever and ever."

They smiled at each other. Dawn's Caribbean blue eyes sparkled in the light of passing cars.

"You okay?" he asked.

"I should be asking you," Dawn said. "You really went after that fire. Did you get burned?"

"I just kept thinking, I'm about to leave and I'm just gonna torch everything behind me? I don't know what I would have done if that — that thing hadn't come along. I couldn't stop it myself."

Dawn shook her head and reached for the curls at Jerry's neck, twisting them lightly around her finger. "Well then, I guess you got a new friend."

2019 – New Jersey

The Barrens were like a bright day under a blanket, muffled, dark and still. Mosquitos buzzed in Andy's ear as he wiped a trickle of sweat from his forehead. Mike held his phone up, ready to record.

"You ready?" Mike asked. The ba-ding of the video record chimed and Andy stood up straight, making his face look serious, stern, like his father's face when he lectured Andy about doing something real with his life.

"Out here in the New Jersey Pine Barrens, residents have long told stories about a monster who lurks in these dark woods. Wait, stop. That isn't what I wanted to say," Andy waved his hand and Mike sighed.

"It's fine, man. Let's just get on with it."

"No, it has to be right. This is our shot, dude. We need to get it right. Let's go again."

"There's a bug on your forehead," Mike said as he deleted the video and turned the phone back toward Andy.

"Damn it!" Andy smacked his head and brought away a black and bloody smear. "Is there a welt?"

"I thought you liked bugs," Mike said.

"Yes, they're important to the ecosystem but I don't want them biting me," Andy grumbled, rubbing his forehead with spit until it came up clean. "This is Monster Corner, Mike. A freaking national show. This needs to look professional."

"An internet show," Mike corrected him.

"With a national audience, and the best shows get picked up by Monster Planet for streaming services. Our last one was so close to making it. We gotta get this one right. No mess-ups this time. Do I look okay? Do I have a welt?"

"It's fine." Mike rolled his eyes and raised the phone again. "And we're on in three, two, one..."

"In New Jersey there are over a million acres of dark, sandy, pine forests. It is protected by legislation to preserve this unique wilderness and shelters a monster that locals call...The Jersey Devil."

Mike gave him a thumbs-up but Andy was feeling it now. He strolled carefully to a warped pitch pine. "Many New Jersey residents have stories about the Jersey Devil. They say it has stalked them through the woods, knocked over canoes in the creeks that run through the Barrens, and even peered at them through the windows of their home. There are many ideas about where it comes from and what it wants but they aren't truly sure of anything except that the Jersey Devil is very real. And that, my friends, is what my cameraman, Mike Grossman, and I, Andy Kreiger, intend to prove."

Andy leaned up against the blackened trunk of the pine. Mike zoomed on the twisted part of the tree that looked like a monstrous face and then stopped the camera. "Cut. Perfect. All right. I'm sorry about giving you a hard time. That was a much better take."

"I told you," Andy said. "C'mon. Let's get some shots and then I gotta meet Becky for dinner."

"Dude, I thought we were shooting through the night. I brought my night vision lens."

"Tomorrow," Andy said. "She's already mad that I'm here instead of at some stupid spa with her."

"Tell her to meet us here. I have to visit my grandma tomorrow night."

"I told you we shoot day shots today, do the first night investigation tomorrow and then interviews on Thursday. Then we gotta determine if we have enough to do a whole show."

"You didn't tell me any of this. I got other shit to do. I got this week off to visit with family. I can only shoot between family stuff."

"I told you the schedule. You never freaking listen, you know."

Mike glowered at him and Andy knew it was time to back off. He wished he didn't need Mike but he did.

Mike was a pushover most of the time, but when he dug in his heels, Andy was not going to get his way. He'd hoped he could convince Mike on this, so he could deal with Becky, who was also pissed at him for supposedly changing their plans.

"Fine, everyone's mad at me. What about tomorrow morning? Can we reschedule the interviews for then? Will your grandma approve?"

"My grandma is in hospice, asshole. You know that," Mike grumbled. "But yeah. Fine."

"Awesome. So let's do some daytime shots now. Okay?"

Mike shrugged and they both pressed record on their phones and started on the narrow path through the woods, their steps deadened by the blanket of pine needles over the rich and spongey ground.

"Did you ever see the Jersey Devil?" Mike asked Andy as they walked through the softened silence of the Barrens. He was good at this, knowing that they could use clips of relevant conversation in their show later.

"I never did, but I moved out of Jersey when I was a kid. I heard stories growing up, though. We all did, I guess."

"Yeah, my sister said she saw it once. It had legs like a deer, but it stood upright and it had wings," Mike said. "She was taking a hike with her friends and she said they felt like something was watching them. When they stopped to eat, she said the forest got really still and then kinda cold and then suddenly they saw this—this thing come leaping out at them.

It was so fast they hardly had a chance to realize what it was and then it was flying past them and into the woods again. She was really freaked out."

"We've heard a lot of stories like that," Andy said. "I wonder what the Jersey Devil wants and why he would bother following a group of hikers."

They walked a bit longer, panning along a wide creek that rolled lazily through the forest, its waters the color of dark tea. They got a shot of a massive dragonfly, the size of Andy's hand, and then Andy saw it was time to head back, or face Becky's ire.

Andy was watching the path through the screen of his phone when it went black.

"Dude, I just charged it on the way here." He punched at the power button. "It was a hundred percent."

"I still got about fifty percent." Mike cracked open a bottle of water and chugged it down.

"Well, I guess get some shots of me walking ahead. I'm gonna hear it from Becky when I don't text."

"Don't even complain, dude," Mike said. "She always lets you off the hook."

Mike tossed his water bottle onto the ground and focused his phone on Andy.

"Dude," Andy said.

"What?" Mike asked.

"Pick that up! The ground isn't your freaking trash can."

Mike rolled his eyes. "Damn, you're such a pain in my ass."

"I just don't think you should be littering out here." Andy felt a blush coming on. He had few strong views, but dumping trash was one of them. The Pine Barrens were hot and buggy and weirdly silent, but they were clean, pristine nature and he didn't want to see that destroyed.

Mike picked up the water bottle and tossed it at Andy, who caught it, crushed it and put it in his pocket. It might look funny in shots, but it was better than leaving it here.

Andy tried to look handsomely pensive for the shot as he walked ahead of Mike, but he was irritated. Not just at Mike. He'd told Becky he would only be out for an hour. They'd rolled into Sea Isle last night for a weeklong vacation, and she had wanted to spend the day together.

He hadn't really been completely clear with her how much work he needed to do. Or even what the work was. He didn't think she'd take him seriously if he told her he was trying to get an episode on Monster Corner. Or she'd make fun of him like his dad always did.

Only Mike shared Andy's obsession with real monsters. They'd met on a Monster Corner forum, but Mike was a dork. Andy was not.

A shadow dashed across the path ahead of him.

"Was that a deer?" he asked Mike.

"What?" Mike asked.

It ran across the path again, just around the bend. It didn't quite look like a deer.

He ran and expected Mike to be right behind him. There was the shadow again and now Andy saw it was tall, really tall, and it was flitting in and out of the woods, fast, across the path.

"Mike, are you getting this?" he shouted over his shoulder.

"Andy! Hold up!" Mike was farther behind him than he should have been. Andy couldn't stop though. He saw the fold of leathery wings, the hooved feet, the large, goat-like head, and it was just ahead of him, moving so fast. Then it was gone. Had he imagined it? Where had it gone? And where the hell was Mike?

Andy let out a deep sigh and decided to go back to his car to wait. He turned, right into the Jersey Devil.

The creature was tall, much taller than anyone had ever suggested. Nine feet maybe? It loomed over him, glaring down with wet brown eyes. Its body was covered in thin fur, deer's fur, from its chest to its legs, but its arms were long, naked, clawed, and almost humanlike. It had a long snout, bristled in grayish fur, but it wasn't like a deer's face and its expression was almost human, with deep brows furrowed into something that looked like sorrow. Two long horns curled back from its skull, yellowed and scuffed, and a long slender tail whipped from side to side behind it.

"I—uh—I—uh—Mike!" Andy screamed. Then its great wings expanded, wide, membrane thin, and really rather beautiful. It flapped them and took off up into the trees, leaving only a trail of waving pines in its wake.

"Mike!" Andy cried again and Mike stumbled out of the forest.

"Geez, man! You took off so fast. What the hell were you thinking?"

"You didn't catch it? You didn't catch any of it?" Andy almost wept.

"Catch what?"

"The Jersey Freaking Devil! He was here, man. He was here and you — you — you... Oh my God!"

Andy buried his face and sank to the ground. His heart pounded so hard he thought he might be having a heart attack, but no. This was just the culmination of his entire life's work. Wasted.

"You saw it?" Mike asked. "Cool. So at least we know we're really looking for something."

"If it's not on camera..." Andy couldn't even look at Mike. "It might as well not exist."

New Jersey – 1969

Dawn huffed when she answered the phone. "Where have you been all day? I've been calling."

"I know." Jerry sighed. He couldn't seem to get his act together. "I'm sorry, baby. I just — I just..."

"The Pine Barrens? Again?"

"I was talking to some people over at Mick's Shop. Everyone there had a story about the Jersey Devil and they all think that he — "

"Jerry, we're supposed to be leaving for San Francisco in a week. We have so much to do. My mom keeps telling me you're getting cold feet."

"Aw, honey, no. Never. I love you. I can't wait to be with you in sunny California, playing music and — "

"Then you need to cut this out, baby," Dawn said. "I know we had something crazy happen to us, but we're trying to leave Jersey behind. We need to be looking toward the West Coast now. Do you feel me?"

"Baby, yes, I do, but...I just need to go out there one last time. I just need to follow this lead Mick gave me. Just this one last time."

"Fine. Then I'm coming with you."

"No, babe, it's gonna be buggy and dirty and — "

"Jer, do you think I care?" Dawn said. "I want to be with you. No matter where you are. In New Jersey or San Francisco or Siberia. So you pick me up tomorrow before you go wherever you're going. Okay?"

Jerry took a deep breath. "Okay. Yeah. All right. Just, you know, wear your bug spray."

New Jersey – 2019

Andy took a long drink of his beer. The little beachside restaurant was packed and he'd kept Becky waiting, fighting to keep their table. She was pissed, just as he expected.

"It was a work thing." He shrugged.

"Why can't you just tell me what the work thing is?" she asked. "I mean, I get that your phone died but why didn't you call me from Mike's phone? Why won't you tell me what you guys are working on?"

It was always the same. Andy would be just a little late and Becky would lose her shit. He took another sip.

"Look, I'm here now. Can we just enjoy the night? Mike's already mad at me because he wanted to work tonight."

"What were you going to do tonight?" Becky asked.

"We're filming. You know I can't talk about it."

"Why the hell not?" Becky asked. "You're not in the CIA, Andy."

"It's the process," Andy said. "It just doesn't work when too many people are involved."

Becky took a long drink from her margarita. Her tone was tight but pleasant when she spoke again. "Did you have a productive day?"

Andy wished he could tell her how productive his day had been. That he'd come face to face with the Jersey Devil and that freaking Mike had missed it all. He wished he could tell her, but he didn't dare. Becky didn't have a weird thing about her. In college she'd turned down an internship for a sci-fi show because "it was not her thing." She was beautiful, ambitious, and from a great family who supported her. She liked normal stuff like baseball and the news. Monsters were not even in her scope.

"It was fine," he said. "You know."

"I missed you today. Are you gonna have a chance to hang out with me at all this week? I mean, I thought this was our vacation."

"Yeah, I can hang out. I've got tomorrow night free and all of Thursday," Andy said, but he was already thinking. Maybe he should get down to the Pine Barrens alone. Bring a couple cameras in case they started to die on him again. There was no reason his phone should have died today. Especially not before Mike's. Maybe Mike was a liability. Maybe he should see what he could get without him. He didn't need Mike to make this happen. He just needed proof. Himself and proof.

"We'll go to the beach tomorrow?" Becky asked.

"Yeah, for a little bit," Andy said. "Then I gotta do some work, but I'll take you out tomorrow night."

"Can't I help you with any of it?" Becky asked. "I mean, I do work in film too. I might be able to help."

"Becks, I just want you to see the finished product. I don't want you to worry about working while we're here. Go to the boardwalk and go shopping or something while I'm out."

Becky's face pinched. "Go shopping. Is that what you think I do when you're not around? Like, that's my only interest?"

"It was just a suggestion." Andy shrugged.

Becky shook her head. "I think maybe I should just go home. This is not the vacation I thought it would be. Maybe that's my fault but you know what, Andy? After two and a half years, I don't think it's out of line to want to know what my boyfriend is working on, or to want to spend time with him when we go away together."

"Whoa, Becky." Andy grabbed her wrist as she tried to push past the table. "You are losing your mind over this little thing. I just need a few hours of filming here and there. And if you need to know about the project, it's the Pine Barrens. I wanted to surprise you when it was done, but there it is. So that's what I'm doing all day. Trekking through that wilderness, getting eaten by mosquitos and arguing with Mike. But it's a big paying job if we do it right so I gotta do it."

He pulled a yellow rose from his bag. "Look. I was thinking of you."

Andy had made an emergency stop on his way here just to get it. He'd given her a yellow rose when he'd asked her out in college, and it had become their thing, and his go-to when he wanted to get out of a fight.

Becky pressed her lips together as she accepted the rose, sinking back down into her seat.

The truth was that Andy was crazy about this girl, but Becky was on the fast track to success with an assistant producer job for a big show, and she'd been talking for a while about getting a place together. Andy's full-time job editing training videos had him planted solidly in his dad's basement of disapproval.

Getting his show picked up for Monster Corner would have helped him start making a name for himself. Getting a shot of the actual Jersey Devil, though, that was a game changer. He wouldn't just be a struggling freelance filmmaker. He'd be famous and getting out of Dad's house would only be the start of the big changes.

Becky didn't know it, but his success this week was going to mean their success as a couple.

New Jersey – 1969

The forest enveloped them, blocking out the sounds of the highway and the glaring light of the summer day. In spite of the thick coat of bug spray Jerry and Dawn wore, the mosquitos were on them in swarms and their sweaty arms were covered in welts and black and red smears.

"Mick said the path is right up here," Jerry said. "You okay, baby?"

"I'm fine," Dawn replied, although rather irritably. Jerry knew she'd rather be on the beach with their friends or maybe spending time with her mom. Although Dawn and her mom didn't really get along well, it was going to be hard for Dawn to leave her. Jerry didn't have that problem. His mom was long gone and he didn't see his dad, a fisherman, enough to not get along, or really have any relationship at all.

"Here it is." Jerry forgot his reservations as soon as the forest opened up to the trail. It was barely more than a deer path, a narrow strip of well-trod earth, the pine needles forming mounds on either side. "Mick said there's an old cabin just a few miles in where he found a bunch of weird stuff when he was a kid."

"What kind of weird stuff?" Dawn asked, smacking another fat mosquito from her arm.

"I dunno. He said it was, like, lost things. Socks. A really old tobacco pipe. Newspapers and old books."

"And what does this have to do with the Jersey Devil?" Dawn asked.

Jerry heard a twig snap in the dark forest and peered into the heavy gloom. Another twig snapped and he caught sight of the tall form. His heart jumped in his chest and then the creature stepped out into the light.

"A deer," he muttered and kicked a clod dirt.

"Jer, what does this cabin have to do with the Jersey Devil?" Dawn asked again.

"I don't really know. Mick said the kids used to say the cabin was where Mother Leeds locked him away after he was born."

"Mother Leeds?"

"You've heard that old story. The woman found out she was pregnant with her thirteenth child and she said 'Let this one be the devil' and the baby was born a devil. I thought everyone knew that story."

Dawn shrugged. "I guess I heard it, but it always sounded stupid to me. Do you believe it?"

"No." Jerry scanned the woods. He didn't hear anything besides the large doe that was still grazing nearby but he felt something. Eyes on him. He looked up in the canopy of pine boughs over them. "No, I don't think that thing we saw was a devil. When he looked at me, it was like, I don't know how to describe it, Dawn. It was like he understood me or something."

Dawn didn't say anything and Jerry stole at glance at her face. Her blue eyes were dark, troubled, as she regarded the path ahead of them.

They walked for a long time. The forest around them grew darker. Dawn tied her blonde hair back and had given up on smacking at the mosquitos. Her arms were covered in angry red welts.

"This is stupid," Jerry said. "We should head back. It's going to be dinnertime before we get back to the car and your mom is going to be mad at me."

"A little further, babe," Dawn said, reaching out and taking his hand. "We already came all this way."

Jerry felt a painful ache of gratitude, love, and guilt in his heart. He promised himself that he would treat Dawn like the queen she was every day after this.

After another mile, however, he was struck with the gnawing urge to really turn around. They were in the heart of the Pine Barrens now and the mosquitos had stopped biting. The birds had stopped singing and the temperature had dropped a good ten degrees. It should have felt more comfortable but Jerry felt jittery, with a growing strangeness in his limbs. The feeling of being watched was so strong now that his eyes darted from shadow to shadow, expecting to see those luminous eyes, those leathery wings.

"Let's head back," he said. "I want to go home."

"Look!" Dawn cried, pointing into the gloom ahead of them.

A murky stretch of brown-stained marsh water spread out before them, spots of afternoon sunlight reflecting across the still waters, and beside them, buried in the shadows of the tallest, oldest conifers Jerry had ever seen...

"The cabin," he whispered.

It was a plain old thing, built of crumbling stone with a damp, mossy roof and windows black with grime, but it was intact. Completely intact and even more, the path they were on led right up to the rotting front door.

Dawn started toward it but Jerry held tightly to her hand, his feet rooted in the soft spongy earth. "No. No, you shouldn't go in there."

He could almost hear something coming from the dark cracks around the old doorway. A whisper. A call. The hair on his arms stood straight up and he just wanted to get Dawn away from here.

"But Jer, we came all this way." She tugged but Jerry held tight.

"No," he said. "Let's go. We saw it. That's all I needed. Let's go."

Dawn examined his face for a minute as Jerry chewed on his lower lip. The truth was, he wanted to know what was in that cabin. Those whispers, that strange energy seemed to be tugging him toward the door. He needed to know what it was, but more than that, he needed Dawn to be safe. He was sure that she should not go in there.

"Okay." Dawn shrugged. "Maybe after dinner we can go to the beach? Take a swim and dry out all these mosquito bites."

"Yeah." Jerry nodded. Relief flooded through him. He looked back at the cabin. He should never come back here again. He should not. "Yeah, a swim sounds so good. You think your mom will let you out?"

“I’m an eighteen-year-old adult, Jer,” Dawn said, flipping her long ponytail. “She can’t stop me.”

The mood lightened with each step they took away from the cabin, with Dawn and Jerry racing each other on the last mile toward the car. But the further they got from the cabin, the tighter the tug Jerry felt in his heart, calling him back.

He shouldn’t go back.

He should never go back.

New Jersey – 2019

Andy was in a foul mood when he met Mike in front of the little ranch house in the woods. After dinner with Becky, he’d spent the night before chasing shadows in the Pine Barrens, running after every cracking branch and gust of wind. He felt sure the Devil was there, watching him, but he caught no evidence to support this intuition.

He’d awoken exhausted, achy, and itchy as hell, absolutely covered with mosquito bites and Becky was mad again.

“Dude, you wanna do this or not?” Mike asked as Andy glowered at the slightly run-down house of Rita Myner, a long time Pine Barrens resident who had agreed to be their first interview.

“You said you wanted to film last night,” Andy

snapped. "Then you didn't even answer my texts."

Mike rolled his eyes and got out of the car.

No one understood what Andy was up against. A future with Becky, a great job and the fame of being the one who uncovered the Jersey Devil, or oblivion, obscurity and eternity in his dad's basement.

Rita Myner answered the door looking like a little grandma, in a floral housedress and a head full of old pink curlers.

"Oh, I musta lost track of time watching my stories," she cried. "You fellas just make yourselves comfortable. I've got some cookies on the coffee table. Just let me get my hair."

She scurried down the shag-carpeted hall and Mike sat down on the rough plaid couch in front of a crystal plate of cookies on a sturdy, old, round coffee table.

Andy picked up a cookie and sneered. "Generic Oreos," he said.

"Dude, cookies," Mike said and shoved one in his mouth.

Mrs. Myner kept the most cliché old lady house Andy had ever seen, with coarse crocheted, blankets — smelling vaguely of cat pee — draped over the orange and brown couches. Framed embroidered phrases like "Kiss the cook" and "Happy wife, Happy Life" hung on the faux wood paneled wall. Even the TV was an old tube style with the cheap carved wood frame around it.

"Oh good, you found the cookies." Rita Myner smiled brightly as she came back in.

Mike swallowed his cookie. "Thank you very much,

ma'am. And we appreciate you being willing to let us interview you. Do you mind if we film?"

He held up his phone and Rita giggled. "Oh my goodness, with that little thing? You know, this isn't my first interview about the Devil. But back then they had to make several trips to bring in all the equipment to film me."

"Let's get started, Mrs. Myner." Andy had no patience for her reminiscing.

Rita Myner, it turned out, had lived in the Pine Barrens her entire life and encountered the Jersey Devil at least four times during that very long life.

"There were a few times it could have been that bugger, but I just couldn't be sure. Rattling at my windows, and my poor cat, Sissy...something ate her in the woods. But I only saw him for sure four times. Once when I was a girl. He walked right out of the woods while I was playing on my porch. Walked across the yard and into the woods again. Then again, when I was a young woman. That time was the scariest. I was out necking with a boy, near the woods, and he just jumped out, flapping those awful wings of his and screeching. Near gave me a heart attack, and that boy, well he just took off running. Didn't ever go out with him again."

"Mrs. Myner, did the Jersey Devil ever threaten you, or seem like he might hurt you?" Andy asked.

"Nope. Never. Fact, I only ever heard of him hurting one person. Man just disappeared in the woods looking for him, must have been nearly forty years ago."

"Really? Was he ever found? How do you know it

was the Jersey Devil who got him?" Andy asked, sitting up straight.

"Well, I can't say nothing for sure, dear. But you should talk to my neighbor, Dawn DuLac. It was her fella at the time, and she was the one who said the Devil took him."

"Could you, uh, introduce us?" Andy asked.

"Oh, certainly dear. I'll call her right now." Rita bustled into the kitchen. Andy was pretty sure his eyes bulged when she pulled the handpiece from a rotary phone on the wall and started turning the numbers.

"Dude," Mike hissed. "What are you doing? We didn't even hear the rest of her stories."

"I have a feeling about this," Andy said. "Trust me."

Mike huffed. Andy was pretty sure that once they were done shooting today, he and Mike would not be working together again.

Mrs. DuLac was as different from Rita Myner as a woman could be, although she herself was not young. With long, silvery blonde hair and a nice figure, flattered by her jeans and t-shirt, she was one of the most attractive older women Andy had ever seen.

"Rita tells me you're doing a documentary on the Devil," she said as she sat on the sofa beside Mrs. Myner. "I don't know if I can be much help. I only saw him the one time."

"We're interested in hearing about your—er—friend who disappeared," Andy explained, turning his camera on to film her.

Mrs. DuLac pressed her lips together and took

a deep breath. "Jerry. My fiancé. We were going to move to San Francisco together, get married. A few days before we were supposed to leave, he went into the woods, looking for the devil, and he was never seen again."

"And you think the Jersey Devil got him?" Mike asked.

"We both saw him, at a party in the woods, but Jer looked him in the eyes. He became obsessed. Wouldn't stop until he found him again. I don't know why. But I know he found him."

"How do you know?" Mike asked.

"Jerry and I grew up here. He knew those woods like the back of his hand. He wouldn't have gotten lost, wouldn't have done something stupid like getting trapped in the marshes. And we loved each other. He would have done anything to come back to me."

"How long ago was this?" Andy asked.

"Fifty years, I guess," Mrs. DuLac said. "Long time."

Andy thought Mrs. DuLac had some great genetics to still look so good in her late sixties.

"Did you ever go to San Francisco?"

She smiled sadly and shook her head. "No. My daughter lives in L.A. now. Been out to see her a few times. Every year since my husband died. But never San Fran. That was supposed to be me and Jerry's place. I just…I could never go, never leave without him."

"Mrs. DuLac, is there anything you can tell us about where Jerry might have gone to look for the Jersey Devil? Any path you could direct us to?"

She looked hard at Andy. Her eyes were a brilliant

shade of blue, and she pressed her lips together into a tight line. She shook her head. "No. No idea."

New Jersey – 1969

In three days, Jerry and Dawn would be on their way to California. They were just waiting for Jerry's dad to come into port and the little goodbye party Dawn's mom was throwing. Then their lives would be perfect, forever.

There was no reason for Jerry to be thinking of the Jersey Devil, as he stood on the precipice of his entire future.

But he couldn't get it out of his head.

At night, he dreamed of the cabin in the woods.

During the day, he'd zone out to find himself driving toward it, miles off course.

And he would jolt forward, at odd moments, full of panic that the Pine Barrens were in peril.

"Baby, I think you're getting sick." Dawn felt his forehead when he arrived at her mother's peeling yellow rancher near the bridge to Ocean City.

"I'm fine," he said, catching her hand and bringing it to his lips. "Just not sleeping well."

"You're still thinking about that cabin, aren't you?" Dawn's blue eyes were the color of a stormy ocean.

"No." He shook his head a little too forcefully and

Dawn frowned.

"In a few days we'll be far away from the Pine Barrens and any monsters that live there," she said, ignoring his lie. Jerry blushed. He never lied to Dawn. She was too good for him.

He tried to help her pack, but he kept returning to the little window in her bedroom to stare out over the gray waters of the inlet, just visible through the houses across her street. The air stank with exhaust and factory runoff. What would New Jersey turn into once they were gone? Would all the beaches become landfills? Would the forests burn to the ground? Would the creatures that relied on this land wither away? The fish his father had spent his life reeling in slowly sink to the bottom of the sea?

He thought of the Jersey Devil that night they met, stomping on the errant flames, glaring into Jerry's eyes.

You did this, his eyes had said. *You need to fix it.*

"Jerry!" Dawn's voice cut through his dark thoughts and her hand wrapped gently around his arm. He jumped and spun toward her, his heart pounding with fear of something he couldn't explain.

"Baby," she whispered, wrapping her arms around his waist. "Go home and sleep. I'll see you tomorrow, before the party."

"Dawn, I — "

"Jerry," she interrupted him, taking his face in her hands. "I love you. Please take care of yourself and get your head on straight. If you're having any doubts..."

"No," Jerry barked. "Dawn, no doubts. I love you so

much. I just want to spend my life with you. Anywhere you want to be."

But that wasn't all he wanted. Jerry knew she could sense it, the rope pulled taut around his chest, pulling him back toward the cabin.

He kissed her goodbye and got into his car, driving past the gravel road to his own house and onto the Garden State Parkway, toward the Pine Barrens.

New Jersey – 2019

Andy sullenly endured the morning shopping with Becky on the boardwalk, but after a half hour she stopped trying to talk to him. He knew he was glum, but she could have at least been a little understanding. He'd told her he hit a wall with his project, even if he couldn't tell her what the project was.

"I'm sorry, Andy, but this is my vacation too and this is the first day you've actually been able to spend with me!" she snapped when she came out of a surf shop to find him leaning over the boardwalk railings, glowering at the sea.

"It's not my vacation," Andy muttered. "It's my entire future."

Becky sighed heavily and reached out to rub his shoulder. He shrugged her off and she recoiled, sucking her quivering lower lip into her mouth.

"Well, it's my vacation, and you asked me to come. My only one all year. I could have used this time to see my family in Michigan, or go to a wedding in New Orleans, but I used it to be with you. And you—you're being a jerk!"

"I'm being a jerk?" he snorted. "All you've done is spend money and whine since we got here."

Becky took a step back, tears quivering in her eyes. "It's my money." She shook her head. "Go to hell, Andy."

She was still shaking her head as she stormed down the boardwalk toward their hotel.

Andy groaned, leaning over the railing. He'd give her time to cool off. Then he would take her out for lunch or something, try to keep his foul mood in check. He wished that she could support him, understand how important this was to him. But that was girls. They were all about feelings and support until you needed it reciprocated.

Someone had knocked over a trash can on the beach and Andy's mood got darker. Was it so hard to just take care of your garbage? This was the beach! A natural habitat for millions of creatures! People were such pigs!

He was picking up the trash, with no help from anyone else, when his phone rang. He expected to see Becky's name on the screen but it was a number he didn't know. He answered anyway.

"Is this Andy?" a woman asked.

"Yes, and this is?"

"Dawn DuLac," she said. "Listen...I've been thinking

about this since I talked to you. I didn't want to tell you because, well, Jerry never came back. If we hadn't found that damned cabin...I think my life would have been very different. You have to understand, it could be dangerous, but I feel like if anyone can reveal this monster, it's you. You seem really dedicated."

Andy gaped for a moment, his heart hammering in his chest, before he managed to say, "Cabin? Yes! Yes, I am. It's — Mrs. DuLac, it's all I really want!"

She sucked in a breath. "That's what I thought. I'm going to text you the coordinates of the cabin, the best I can remember it. But Andy, please — please be careful. Jerry didn't know what he was getting into, going out there. Please protect your — "

"Thanks, Mrs. DuLac, I'll be fine. I'll make sure you get proper credit in the show."

"Andy — "

She said something else but he just grunted and said goodbye as he rushed to pick up the last of the trash.

He dashed to the florist near the boardwalk and got a rose that was more orange than yellow, but good enough. He called Mike on the way to the hotel but the bum didn't pick up his phone. Typical.

"Hey, Becky. Something came up," he called as he entered the hotel room to change. "I've gotta run out, but when I come back, I'll take you out to celebrate. Anywhere you want. The project is back on track and I have something big. Oh, and I got you something."

Becky didn't answer and he pulled a fresh shirt

over his head and looked around the room. She wasn't there. Neither was her suitcase.

"Fine." He tossed the rose in the trash. "It's just me then."

He seethed as he drove toward the Pine Barrens. He was doing this FOR Becky. For them to have a future together. But maybe he'd dodged a bullet. Becky was selfish, putting her time and her career over him and his dreams. She thought she was too good for him because of her job. She didn't believe in him. When he caught the Jersey Devil on video, it would be his accomplishment. Not hers. Not Mike's. He'd start a new life, hosting his own monster show. He'd have better girls to pick from. He'd leave them all in the dust.

He was lucky to see the overgrown turnoff, which was obscured with pine boughs and brambles, but just clear enough for him to pull in. His tires were nearly silent on the bed of pine needles coating the ancient gravel and the darkness of the forest was immediate. He parked where the drive turned to a narrow deer path, his anger at Becky and Mike fading as the Barrens beckoned him. The only thing that mattered was at the end of that path.

New Jersey – 1969

The party was cancelled. The police were called. Jerry's father came into port early. The day of the big escape across the country came and went but Jerry had disappeared.

Dawn could have directed the police to the cabin, but she didn't. She needed to see for herself first. She needed to know for sure what she felt in her heart.

New Jersey – 2019

Evening was edging in when Andy finally arrived at the cabin, hidden in the long black shadows between glaring spots of setting sunlight. His arms were raw from itching bug bites. His eyes stung from sweat and his clothes clung to him. He was pretty sure he was emitting a cloud of BO that was attracting every bug in the Pine Barrens.

But here it was and something in the deepest part of his core seemed to crack open and reach for it.

The cabin was small, but tidy, with freshly mortared stone and a new cedar shingle roof. A little chimney piped out a thin curl of smoke that ribboned through the streams of sunlight, reaching for Andy. It smelled earthy and sweet and the insects around him ceased their unrelenting feast on his skin at last.

"Welcome home," Andy muttered and then blinked, unsure why he had said it. He felt warm inside, a peace settling in his heart and compelling his limbs forward, toward the freshly painted green door.

There was a shuffle inside and Andy paused, his hand hovering over the doorknob. What did he expect to find here? That the Jersey Devil was chilling in a little hunting cottage in the middle of the woods, gardening and chopping wood?

It didn't matter. No reasoning could stop that tug in Andy's chest, that call in his heart, that feeling that he was finally exactly where he belonged.

Instead of turning the knob, he knocked. There was another shuffle from inside and then the knob turned and a man opened the door.

He was disappointingly ordinary looking, in a gray t-shirt and a pair of red sweat shorts, his gray hair a bit shaggy for an old dude, and a trim goatee that still had streaks of dark brown in it. But his eyes, they locked onto Andy's. They were wide and brown and Andy recognized them from somewhere.

"If you want to know, there's a price," the man said. "Only come in if you're ready."

"Whatever it is, I'm ready," Andy replied and it was true. He had to know, he had to walk through that door. He didn't care what it cost him.

The man sighed and opened the door wide to admit Andy into the little cabin. There was a plush velvet couch in front of the little fire, a small kitchen, a loft with a big bed, strewn with cushions. It was cozy and inviting, but as soon as Andy walked through the threshold a chill broke out over his skin and then sunk into his already fragile heart.

The man winced. "It's not that bad. Not this part. But there's no going back now. I am sorry. I've been waiting for so long."

"What do you—"

"I'm glad you came, Andy," a woman said behind him and he turned to see Mrs. DuLac, looking pretty in a long hippie dress. "We've waited for so long for Jerry's turn to be over."

"You might be resistant at first. You might be mad." The man, Jerry, said. "I was. Dawn and I had big plans, but as soon as I saw him—well, I knew I was the one to take his place. Just like when you and I met in the woods."

"I, um, I—what?" Andy stammered, his brain reeling, the deep, strange chill settling into his bones. It wasn't uncomfortable though. It felt right. It felt serene. He was understanding in his flesh, even if his brain was struggling to catch up.

"For fifty years I have been the guardian of the Barrens. This land is sacred, a heart in the earth, and it needs to be protected at all cost. It's usually a solitary job, as you can understand. Outside that door, I am not a man. I am something more. But here, in this cabin, I'm Jerry. And Dawn found me here, after I took the role from the last guardian."

"You're the Devil." Andy finally grasped it.

"I was the Devil," Jerry said. "I traveled the Barrens, New Jersey, even further, ensuring the protection of this land. I kept the balance. I kept the heart safe.

Now...you're the Devil. For fifty years you must bear this mantle. Then you will find someone to take your place and your life will be yours again."

"H — How?" was all Andy could utter.

Dawn DuLac wrapped her arms around Jerry and nestled her face into his neck, curling his hair around her finger.

She had sent Andy here for this reason. Not to find out about Jerry. Because she already knew. She had been married, with a kid, and all this time she knew.

"The threshold of the door," Jerry said. "I don't know how it works, only that it's been here for eons. As long as man has walked these lands, it's called for a guardian. And they always come. Dawn and I have been waiting for you for a long time. We made the cabin as comfortable as we can. I think you can be happy here."

Dawn tugged Jerry toward the door. He cringed and shuddered, pulling back.

"It's okay," she said softly. "You're done. We can go now."

Andy was still reeling as Jerry let Dawn pull him out of the cabin. Jerry stood in the evening air, his face turned up to the canopy of trees above him.

"Wait!" Andy realized they were leaving him. Leaving him here with...what? This couldn't be what they said it was. They couldn't do this to him! None of this could be real!

"I wish I could help you more, Andy," Jerry had tears rolling down his face, but Andy thought he looked joyful. "But you're going to have to learn it on your own. The Barrens will show you what needs to be done. You'll feel it in your bones. You probably do already. But my time is over, and I promised Dawn that we would leave New Jersey."

"Our daughter lives in L.A.," Dawn said. "That's our first stop. Then on to San Fran."

"On to San Fran," Jerry echoed and they started off down the darkened path, hand in hand.

Andy ran toward them, but as soon as he passed through the threshold his bones began to buzz. The chill within him expanded like a soft bubble and then turned hot. His skin, his head, his eyes, his nose... everything expanded, sharpened, and the forest around him became bright and vivid.

Frozen in his tracks, his body splitting from his clothes, Andy tried to cry out again to Dawn and Jerry, but his voice was a screech and his wings flapped, sending cold winds down the path toward them.

He heard them start a car, miles away. He heard the squirrels nestle into the trees for the night. He heard the mosquitoes buzz about, looking for a fresh blood meal to feed their young.

He heard everything and he felt the beating heart of the Pine Barrens and, after a while, he flew toward it.

One Year Later

It was an odd sound that woke Becky from the couch, where she had fallen asleep watching reruns again. Sort of a tapping, or scraping sound, coming from somewhere in the living room.

There it was again, the tapping scrape, and Becky was sure it was coming from the window. The apartment was eighteen floors up, nothing should be scraping or tapping at her windows, but then again, she'd only moved in a month ago. She didn't know all the quirks of this apartment yet.

Stretching until her back cracked, she walked over the uneven hardwood floor to the window. It was old, original to the building, which meant it actually opened. She pulled the shade, expecting to find a pigeon or a reckless cat.

Instead Becky found a yellow rose. She stared at it. A perfect yellow rose, its petals fluttering in the summer breeze, sitting on the old brick window ledge, eighteen floors above the sticky Brooklyn sidewalk.

"Hey, babe, you coming to bed?" Her boyfriend, Jeremy, came out of the bathroom and kissed her neck. He smelled like mouthwash and Ivory soap.

"Yeah, in a minute," Becky said, blocking the window until Jeremy disappeared into the bedroom. Then she turned back to the rose. The yellow rose.

She took a deep breath and opened the window.

She jiggled the old metal screen until it was up just enough for her to slide her hand beneath it. When her fingers found the velvet smooth yellow petals of the rose, she pushed it off the ledge, to the street below.

Becky shut and locked the window, pulled the shade and went to bed.

Under My Skin

H. A. Callum

Nothing is original anymore. Eleanor's bare feet skimmed the rusted floorboards of the old pickup. With each pulse of the gas pedal, fire crackled from the broken exhaust manifold, toasting her soles, and sending a whiff of half-spent gasoline into the cab. Here she was, in her flip-flops and cut-off jean shorts, riding along with Joel, her Saturday night standby, down the old county road flanked by corn and fence posts. Utter Americana, and she was playing the part.

Eleanor glanced over to Joel, who was tethering the steering wheel with one hand and inching his other hand toward her.

This night was going to be different.

"Pull over," Eleanor said.

"Why?" Joel asked.

"This is it. Where the Jersey Devil was spotted."

A sliver of worn shoulder welcomed the pickup as it crept to a stop alongside an old canal bordering the Turnbaugh property.

"Right," Joel snickered. "Some old farmer loses a cow and suddenly there's a devil on the loose. You need to get away from this place."

"And you don't? Anyway, there's a story in this. I could work it into one of my assignments at the paper. So, man up."

"Besides," Eleanor went on, "it wasn't a cow. And it isn't an old farmer living there. The new owner isn't much older than us, and he's breeding thoroughbreds. Racehorses, you know, Kentucky Derby, maybe you've heard of that?"

She eased open her door and slid out onto the dew-laden grass. "You coming?"

In answer, Eleanor's flip-flops flew out of the truck's open window and landed at her feet. "Not this time, babe," Joel said. "I'm off to enjoy my Saturday night, not chase ghosts."

He yanked the pickup into drive, gave her a wink, and sped off into the dark country night, the tires spitting gravel at her bare legs.

"It's not a ghost, you dick!" she yelled after the disappearing taillights. "It's a monster!"

She turned toward the property. In the moonless night, the trees shot up like withered fingers scraping their way out of a grave. It was August and there was a chill in the air. The sweat condensed on Eleanor's skin and gave her a slight shiver.

Some *thing* moved through the tree canopy toward her. The treetops parted, swept along by an invisible hand.

Eleanor froze. A scream slipped out of her mouth.

The movement in the trees came to a standstill.

"Can I help you?" a voice asked, as a hand came to rest on her shoulder.

The itch wouldn't go away. It haunted Rick as much as the sounds in the woods, the howls in the night, the silence of his lonely house. What he wanted was someone to share his good fortune with. But this rash, it consumed him, the skin raw from his fingernails raking across it. His eyes turned from his skin to notice a pair of headlights illuminating the towpath of the canal near his property line, possibly more locals out to see if the stories were true. That a monster had visited the property and feasted on one of his pregnant mares. One horse down, and the rumors began churning again. He recalled why he was so eager to leave this place after college. Obviously, things hadn't changed. He'd pissed off his old man by leaving and not carrying on the family tradition. Perhaps Dad would still be here if all that anger hadn't eaten him alive. *If only you could see me now, old man.*

Rick skirted the path that coursed between the house and barn and pushed toward the pasture. Then he saw the outline of a woman, approaching the trees at the far end of the fence line, oblivious to the fact that she was being watched. As her form came into focus, he realized this wasn't teenagers seeking a cheap thrill, as he'd assumed. Why she was out here at night, tooling around, he couldn't guess. He liked the woman as she plowed ahead, fearless. The sound of a vehicle putting distance between itself and the property caught Rick's attention. Was she alone?

Perhaps it was the barn owl, swooping amongst the bats and feasting mid-flight, that caused the woman to look at the trees with closer scrutiny. Rick approached her, but the woman stood there staring through him. He seemed invisible to people sometimes.

And then she screamed. A scream that drowned quickly in the humid summer air. If she were scared, he didn't know why. Rick admired her courage, being out there alone. A woman like her could be just what this place needed.

Rick paused and saw the woman's body silhouetted against a break in the trees. She was frozen in place, too scared to move. He knew that feeling. He felt it nearly every night of his childhood when the woods came to life and the trees would bend to some capricious hand and the night air would be split by howls from another world.

He came up from behind her. She didn't seem to hear his heavy footsteps swishing through the calf-high grass doubled over with dew. The crickets quit playing their songs in deference to his advance. He placed his hand on her shoulder. "Can I help you?"

As his hand came to rest on her, he watched as she turned to face him, almost in slow motion. He watched as her eyes walked the sharp, chiseled lines of his face, his best features he mused. Perhaps it would take her attention away from the rash, which had crawled down his hand. He focused his attention on the woman as her eyes moved from the handsome features of his face, to his hand, and back to his face. Her body tensed. He captured her with a smile that broke from a corner of his mouth and gradually crested to reveal a full set of perfect, white teeth. First impressions count the most.

"It's okay," he said, trying to reassure her. "I'm Rick Turnbaugh. This is my property. I heard something out here." He dropped his hand from her shoulder and offered to shake her hand.

She met him with silence. And a stare at the rash.

"Look, I'm not mad that you're trespassing. I just wanted to make sure everything was okay out here, and then I saw you."

"I ... I'm so sorry. I didn't mean to bother you. It's just that ..."

He noticed her looking over his shoulder, probably toward the road where he'd heard the vehicle leaving just before this event climaxed.

"Mr. Turnbaugh, I'm sorry for all the trouble. Oh, and I'm Eleanor. Eleanor Mays." She extended her hand out to him, and he shook it. He was gratefully surprised by her gesture. She had a firm, commanding handshake and her skin felt warm and fluid, velvet to the touch, pulsing with life. Yes, she would do.

"Just so you know, this was kind of a professional visit. Uninvited, I know. And I hope you'll forgive that.

I write for *The Hunterdon Journal*, just across the river in New Jersey. So, Saturday night, nothing happening, need a story idea, and here I am."

"Hey, it's no problem. And call me Rick. Let's head back to the house. Watch your step, this is a working farm you know?" He smiled and watched a small grin brush across her face, scattering the worry that had been camped there.

"So, you out here all alone?" he asked.

"Yeah, well, my date tonight, let's just say he wasn't the adventurous type."

At that, there was a brief, awkward silence. The light from the farmhouse illuminated the rash, which had also spread to his neck. He caught her staring. "Psoriasis," he said. "Always flares up in the summer. I can't wait for the weather to break."

"Sorry ... I really didn't mean to — "

"No worries, I'm used to it. Anyway, out here to chase monsters tonight?"

"You're from here, so you know."

"If you ask me, monsters get a bad rap. If it were a coyote, or some other predator, it's the circle of life and all is good. But a monster gets hungry and all bets are off. Everyone's gotta eat." He let out a laugh, and she followed.

"Well, you have me there. But losing a horse of that value, I mean, that is a story."

"Yeah, but I don't think there are monsters in the woods. And if there are, at least they're not hungry now."

"Well, monster or no monster, I think it's a story."

"I see. Well, maybe next time you could ask?" He smiled genuinely.

There was something about his smile that transcended the basic laws of attraction. She looked over the pasture and back at the tree line.

"Well, then, Rick, may I come back and visit the property, maybe conduct an interview?"

"You have an open invitation. And ... how does tomorrow morning sound to start? We can talk over brunch."

"I think I could work you in tomorrow. Meet me down at the Devil's Elbow. Eleven o'clock?"

"Perfect, I love the Elbow. Now, care for a ride home?" Rick nodded in the direction of his Range Rover.

"I'd love it. Thank you." He escorted her to the SUV and watched as her eyes widened at the sight of the car's interior.

"The next time you see your date, let him know he's a fool." Rick flashed his smile at Eleanor as the Range Rover began to crawl down the property's long driveway. Rick dropped Eleanor off at her house, a neglected bungalow melting back into the earth, and thought, "She's a real keeper. I don't know why anyone would run from her."

The Devil's Elbow is just the place, as they would say, to bend the elbow. Packed onto a peninsula at a ninety-degree jaunt in the Delaware River, it earned its name for the currents that flowed in macabre rhythm below the water's glassy surface. Eleanor looked out over the river before heading inside to meet Rick. The skin of the water belied what waited beneath, and many had gone down, never to rise again.

"My family took refuge with the Quakers, who wanted nothing to do with the Revolution, of course. For religious people, the Quakers had quite the financial clout. So, when my family aligned with them, for better or worse, the locals let them be. We've been on the same piece of land for over 300 years."

"That is some story, Rick," Eleanor said as she jotted down a few notes and twirled the celery stick in her Bloody Mary with her free hand. "But it's not the one we came to talk about." His dawdling backstory felt like evasiveness.

"I know, but a little background can't hurt, can it?"

"True, and as long as we're telling stories, I think I'll have another." She waved down the waitress. "Put it on my tab," Eleanor said.

"Good, because some stories need to be told in their own time. Especially this one."

Eleanor leaned in closer. His straight jawline, the angles of his face contoured by a five o'clock shadow that was as perfectly cultivated as his wavy dark hair — his rugged handsomeness was hard to dismiss. And then there was something about his eyes, bright amber and focused, that led hers to keep step with the tempo set by his voice. Her attention shifted to the rash spreading down his arms, a long-sleeved shirt no longer enough to obscure it from scrutiny. The striations of the rash had the look of healed burns, the skin taut and twisted, the tendons beneath pulling at his skin with each bit of movement. She turned her attention back to her drink as Rick pulled his shirt cuffs down lower and raised his collar to keep the rash out of sight.

"Where were we?"

"The attack. Your horse. We were just getting to that."

"Right. So, it was after two thirty in the morning on the night it happened. It was darker. The haze coming off the river blocked out most of the moonlight. I don't know what it was, but something woke me up. It wasn't natural, I mean, it felt like something was trying to get my attention. You ever get that feeling?"

Eleanor nodded and answered, "Yeah, last night." A shiver spilled from her fingertips, sending ripples across the drink in her hand.

"It was eerie. And I've never told anyone this. We'll go back and walk the pasture where it happened, but for now, just putting this out there is tough. If I were to tell this to the police, they'd say I was crazy."

Eleanor eyed him with curiosity as he paused. His affect was nervous. She even caught him looking around the restaurant to make sure no one was listening in on their conversation.

He continued, "So I came down and stood on the porch outside the kitchen. It overlooks the barn and both pastures. In the upper pasture, at the corner farthest from the house, a wind picked up. Odd, because it was so calm that night. I heard a winnowing, like a horse but different. It was shriller and finished with a deep grunt. I got this chill, and what I thought was the wind parted the trees just outside the fence. Whatever it was, it was moving fast. Problem was, I couldn't see anything there."

His sentence drifted off.

"I saw it, too. Last night. Something moved through the trees. But it was near the tops of the pines, pushing them aside as it — whatever it was — moved around."

She was waiting on him, her eyes locked on his, a captive audience to hear him tell what happened next.

"I don't believe in all those legends and things like that." He paused, and Eleanor nodded, pushing him to continue. "But then I noticed the gate to the pasture open. Fortunately, most of the horses sensed something was wrong and huddled up in the barn. Except for Leddy. She was a great mare, a beautiful paint horse. And when I saw that the gate was open, I immediately thought someone was up to no good. Those horses ... well, you can imagine what they're worth. Especially if they're pregnant. Two for one."

"Have you had problems out there before?" Eleanor asked. She searched his face for clues, for remorse, anything that could spin the story in the right direction. "It is kind of remote, and you are alone."

"No. The occasional hunter straying onto the property, or kids fishing in the canal, but other than that, it's a forgotten place."

"Parts of our area have that feeling of stepping back in time. It's one thing I would miss about living here, even though I'd always dreamed of getting away."

"Same for me," he said. "But it's nice to get away at times ... from here and the city. Living here gives me that — it's the best of both worlds. Why didn't you get out?"

"Life just happens," Eleanor said. "I was on my way but when my mom got sick, I ended up back here. Now, I'm just too old to go back to college."

Her fingers dawdled over her drink and she relished in the fact that he focused all his attention on her, something that, admittedly, she missed. There hadn't been enough of that since her mom got sick.

"At one time, Eleanor, I had a plan. A fine one, I thought, living a professional's dream in NYC. I'd arrived. On the outside it looked great, especially to my mother. But it didn't work. Something was missing. So, I came back. I was tied to this land more than I had known before I left it. It's a part of me. In some ways, it is me."

"Honestly, I don't know why you'd ever want to leave."

"The same reasons you probably wanted to get out of here. Change is good sometimes. And I had to give it a shot. I returned after my father died. Mom, well, she wasn't for it. But in the end, she understood. Still, I knew I had to do it my way. That's why I went with horses."

She nudged his foot with hers under the table and gave him a sideways grin. She watched him melt back into his chair and could see that the fatigue of telling the story and dredging up old family history was catching up with him.

"Let's head to the farm," Rick said. "I think we've covered enough ground here."

A beginning, a middle and an end. All stories have them. But no story is good without a hook. Eleanor was hooked.

"Just amazing," Eleanor said, in awe as they walked the property.

"I admit, it's pretty special," Rick responded. "But I'm a little prejudiced. When I look back, I don't know why I left. But, getting away did make me appreciate it more."

"It's incredible. Like we've just turned back 300 years."

"The solitude makes the place. If these trees, this house, could only tell stories. Imagine what they would say..."

"Well, that's my job. Remove the mystical rumors after what happened to your mare and her foal. That I know I can do."

Eleanor's eyes swept across the expanse of the property. She drank it in, swam in the fragrances of the farm and the pines, and caught herself falling out of step with Rick. The land, she could feel it tug at her.

Rick looked back. His smile, she thought, was like he'd found something he'd wanted for a long time.

"Take all the time you want," said Rick. "Consider this an open invitation. Nights seem to be when things are most interesting. But you know that."

Eleanor was delighted. She looked forward to visiting the property and gaining familiarity with the place. She was also in tune with how the man and the place seemed inseparable as she watched Rick move through the grass that would soon become next winter's hay. Eleanor placed one foot on the bottom rail of the fence to the pasture. Her eyes squinted and her shoulders tucked inward, anticipating what was to come.

"Let's go in," Rick said, extending his left arm toward the pasture to welcome Eleanor through the gate. The farmhouse stood behind them, casting a mid-afternoon shadow over the quaking grass. To their left was the barn, its history recorded by the gouges and pockmarks etched into its stone walls. The planks above the stones were a weathered gray, far from the traditional red seen everywhere else. The horses watched with interest as they made their way toward them.

"Right, I came out of the kitchen, and headed along the porch that wraps around the house and faces the barn. That's when I saw what I thought was the wind blowing over in the corner of the pasture."

"You were inside when you first heard the sounds?"

"I was. There was no way to not hear them, they were so shrill. Imagine the high-pitched whine of a television with the sound down, then amplify it. My ears felt like they were going to bleed."

"I know that sound. I kind of hear it now, in the background."

"Yes, background noise, but that isn't the same," Rick said. "That's the sound of the place uninterrupted. Crickets. Cicadas. The wind. Combined, those sounds can be deafening at times, too. Be still."

Eleanor closed her eyes and became lost in the cacophony of sound bathing the property.

"Show yourself!" Rick cried out as loud as possible, his voice knocking Eleanor out of her placid interlude.

"Rick!"

"Now, listen. Hear that? That is silence. No crickets. Our presence, my voice, the intrusion, it shut them down. Just like whatever was here that night shut them down. In between the screams was the sound of silence you're hearing now. Let me ask you this, how does it make you feel?"

Eleanor turned her eyes away from that stare of his as he waited for her to respond. She shivered and looked back towards the trees.

"It's a little unnerving," she said.

"You really don't know what lonely is until you hear it. This place at night can get very lonely. You need to be ready for that if you ever decide to stop by after dark."

Eleanor nodded. Her body was rigid, and her eyes were locked on his lips, reading them, as if she had gone deaf in the silence that followed their exchange.

She followed Rick as he headed farther into the pasture, toward the place where Leddy had been killed. "So, I get into the pasture and I notice the two sets of tracks. One's obviously Leddy, and the other looked more like a track made by a large deer."

"But that isn't too odd, is it? I mean, deer can be in the pasture any time. It's not a stretch."

"It is when you consider that there were only two hoof prints from this deer," Rick responded. "Ever seen a deer walk that far on two legs?"

"I was looking exactly in this direction last night," she said. "I was on the other side of the fence, but this is nearly the same line of sight I had coming up the hill. Right there — in that stand of pines on the other side of the fence — was where I saw the trees moving. Their tops were brushed aside like something was moving between them, pushing off each one, as it made its way back into the woods."

"And right by the base of those trees is where I found her," Rick said. "She was right there." They walked over. "On the other side of the fence."

"How — "

"Don't know. That's for you to maybe find out. Anyway, I swept my flashlight over the pasture and saw a pair of tracks leading out toward the gate. One was Leddy's and the other, like I said, wasn't from any animal I know."

"I followed the tracks to Leddy's body and I knelt down beside her. The blood was everywhere, with the spray running ten, fifteen feet up the trunks of the trees. Even worse was the fact that her foal had been cut out of her and was missing."

"You've got to be kidding," Eleanor said. Her entire mood darkened.

"Would I kid about that? It's also the one detail that the police didn't make public. So there's that little scoop for your story. Anyway, I heard rustling in the pines. The boughs of the trees were dancing in its wake. Whoever, whatever it was. So, I'll ask you. How do you explain that to the police?"

"I guess you can't. I mean, I know what you're saying. There wasn't any sign in the woods of whatever it was? No trail to follow?"

"Nothing. When the police came the next day, it was just Leddy and the bloodbath surrounding her. Other than that, there were no tracks in or out. Even the dogs came up with nothing. Not a trace of the foal, either. Like it vanished."

"Listen, Rick. I am so sorry. I didn't know— "

"It's fine. I know you didn't. No one did. All that people were told is that a pregnant horse was killed. No one else knows how. But maybe you can help pin that down."

"When I heard what happened, and the gossip started, I thought it would be an interesting story, you know, local interest, debunk some myths. But this? I don't know."

"Eleanor, this is what you do, right?"

"I guess, but— "

"Then let's dig into this." Rick smiled *that* smile at her.

Eleanor turned to the trees at the murder scene and ran her hands up their trunks, circling each tree as she did. Her eyes followed the stains upward, as if the mare had been brought into the trees before being killed.

"It's her blood," she said.

"Smell it," Rick instructed.

Without questioning his demand, Eleanor brought a bit of the blood-stained bark to her nose. With her free hand she wafted the air, circulating the scent of pine tinged with iron.

"It smells like it looks," he said. "The trees, their tannins, they stain the water that same rust color. The flavor, now that's up for speculation."

Eleanor eyed him, bringing her blood-tinged finger to the corner of her mouth. "I'd imagine they would have a metallic tang countered by the pine's essence. A subtle complexity, like a mushroom."

"So much subtlety," he added in agreement. "Much like life and the people that flavor it."

Eleanor looked at him, then back to the tree. "Some of those stains, they still look fresh."

"It must be the humidity," Rick interrupted. "Or even the tar in the trees, giving it that sheen."

"Let me show you the house before it gets too late." Rick reached out for her hand. Her fingers caressed the striations from the rash that had begun to branch out across his palms. He pulled his hand away.

"It's okay," she said. "It doesn't bother me." She saw pleasant surprise fill his face. Eleanor was warming up to him, despite his oddities. Maybe it was those amber eyes. Sometimes they gave him a kind and unassuming doe-faced look. At other times it gave him the look of a wolf, a wise and loyal wolf.

"No one's ever done that before. I've always been too self-conscious about it."

"Well, don't."

"I'll try not to ... it feels nice."

Eleanor slid her hand deeper into his and nestled her fingers against the creases that covered his palm.

Daylight bled to dusk as they wandered to the old farmhouse. Eleanor was entranced. The history, the old money, this was the yore of an America she once abhorred until getting close to it. Rick wasn't much older than her, and here he was, able to come back here at a young age and live comfortably. That's the gift of old money. An old homestead paid for several hundred times over by the generations that had made their sojourns through life, with this place marking the beginnings of all their stories.

"This is my mother, Rachel." He pointed to a framed photograph in the hall connecting the kitchen to the living room. It was the last in a long line of family portraits that chronicled Rick's lineage. "This farm was actually in her family. They were one of the first families in New Jersey, down along the coast. Some small town, Smithville, I think. Not far from AC."

"Is that your dad?" Eleanor asked.

"That's the old man. He was a local, a farmhand here. It's how he met my mom."

"Such a small-town love story. How original, right?"

"Right." Rick smiled and Eleanor smiled back.

"Anyway, this land was part of the Walking Purchase. Some say it was stolen. This parcel, in fact, was claimed to be part of tribal land up until 2004. But who really owns the land?"

"And your dad didn't have any claim to the land, he just married into it. I'm sorry if I crossed any lines there."

"No, you're right. He walked this property like it was his birthright. I never understood it either." Rick shrugged. "But enough about me. Tell me your story."

Eleanor continued taking in the portraits. And every so often, one of them was housed in a gilded red frame. She did notice that as time wore on, the amount of faces spanning the distance between the unique frames grew. Almost as if there were fewer Turnbaughs being born.

"I suppose it's fair," she said. "But I thought it was me who was interviewing you? Tell me, why are some of these portraits in red frames?"

"I've given you plenty already for at least one story. Please, tell me about you."

She nodded and said, "I guess you're right. It's been a great day, and your hospitality has been wonderful. There's nothing much about me. You have me beat hands down when it comes to family history."

"Don't downplay it. Where your life's headed, that's still a thing of possibility."

"Rick, you know the story. I'm from here. Waited to get out, like you. Didn't and now I hustle writing freelance for the local rag and product descriptions for online retailers. Exciting."

Eleanor knew he was interested in her, trying to learn more about her. She felt it was fair somehow. He had shared a lot about his own family, things he didn't need to share. And the land, it pulled her in. All her life this place had been here, and it wasn't even on her radar. Now that she had experienced the comfort of home and property, she knew she wanted it. Something she had no business wanting from him, or any man. Wasn't she supposed to make her own way?

"The Cliffs Notes version of your life sucks. You can do better. Take me, for example. Remove all this and pretend it's just an old house. Now, look in the living room. See the fireplace? Just to the left, under that window that looks down to the canal, that's where I was born. Home birth, baby. My parents were part of that free love, back to nature movement. Or, if you want, I was the kid with semi-rich parents. Went off to college. Farm life wasn't for me, so I lived in Hoboken and worked in Manhattan. Had a blast. Dad died, and I came home. Boom. End of story. Kind of dull, the second one, isn't it?"

"More like abrupt, I suppose."

"True, it's only lived if you live it. You just told your story like it was an obituary. Take a chance and live. Try it." He grinned and she allowed his eyes to engage her again.

"You have a way with words, don't you?" she laughed.

"No, that's your job, remember?"

"Seems like you've taken it upon yourself already. It feels the other way around."

"Sometimes getting the story takes some prodding. Look, every story has a beginning, a middle, and an end. You know that. But personally, what do you know?"

"About?"

"You. About you. You know your beginning. And the middle, you're probably getting close to it. But the end, now that is left for conjecture." He touched her chin, the ashen skin flaking off from the rash and dusting her shirt.

"I really think I should go. It doesn't feel like much of an interview any longer. Anyway, I think I have enough for now."

"Eleanor, my dad came from nothing. A beginning that wasn't spectacular. But then, by the third act of his life, something shifted. He met my mom. And this, this is how it all ended. Comfort, home, property. You're not much different than him. Can you see what I mean?"

"If you're saying that you and I—"

"I am not saying anything." Rick smiled to lighten the growing tension between them. "But what I was getting at was that your story is still left to be told. Just because you don't find it interesting doesn't mean it can't be."

After saying goodbye to Rick, Eleanor wandered into the pasture and over to the trees where Leddy had met her fate. She ran her hand along the trees, taking time again to rub the dried blood and sap between her fingers, releasing the scent as the friction sent it drifting into the air. It was the essence of life, the marker of death, all in one scent. In the soft light of her phone she looked up at the branches above. Their skeletal fingers reached down, raking at the wind, sending her quickly back to her car parked at the end of the driveway.

The wind rustled and the trees parted eerily. Eleanor frowned but hastily fired up her weathered sedan. The engine roared. Just in time as whatever had been pushing through the trees had begun to swim through the tall grass and wildflowers that filled in the void between the pasture and her car. Eleanor careened onto the road without looking back at whatever had its sights on her.

A week later, Rick heard movement in the pasture. Hooves drummed a deep, bass rhythm in the soft earth that called to him. It was Eleanor, running alongside the horses, smiling like a child at play. Watching her made him want to throw off his shoes and run barefoot. At once he remembered the delight of his childhood, in feeling the blades of grass bend and tickle the bare soles of his feet and send cool drops of dew into the air, saturating his shorts and inking his calves with delicate sprays of muddied earth. That was the connection to this ground that he missed, the part of this place that at one time centered him. He truly felt that, through Eleanor, he had rediscovered this part of himself.

"Good morning. So glad you decided to return."

"I needed some time to think about ... all of this. There's something about here, something that goes beyond what any story could be."

"Well, you're right and wrong." He stopped her momentum, capturing her attention. "There is something about here," he said, and he gestured to the canal, the pasture, and the towering pines. "Nothing goes beyond the story of *here*, of this place."

"I'm sure that rash has a story too," she answered.

"If you only knew, Eleanor." Rick looked into her eyes. "Maybe you do, but you don't want to admit that just yet." He picked at the skin of his palm, sending a long, translucent sheet of flaked skin to the ground. "Fertilizer, ashes to ashes, and all that."

He watched as Eleanor pulled her shoulders in close and wrapped her arms around herself. There was a chill in the air from the shadow of the pines blocking the early morning sun.

Rick eyed her, scanning every inch of her body for a sign. He needed something from her, some indication of what she was feeling. Then he surveyed the property and smiled to himself, grateful for what the place had given him. He scratched his hands, sending shards of dried skin to the mud where they instantly rehydrated and melted back into the ground, disappearing forever.

"So, tell me, Eleanor, what did you really see that first night out here? Do you think monsters are real?"

"It was nothing. Monsters aren't real."

"Maybe they're just not what you think they are."

He inched closer as she took a few steps back to distance herself from him.

"Tell me, what did it look like to you?" Rick asked.

"It was dark. Everything was in silhouette," she said softly.

"But Eleanor, I thought you said that you only saw the trees moving? I think we should discuss this for your story. And I need to know what is out there. Don't you want to know?"

"I can't stay long."

"Some writer, giving up the lead on a story that could really make a difference in your career. Come back when you're ready. But first, we need to clear the air a little more. Who was with you that first night?"

"What does that have to do— "

"I think you should see this." Rick led her closer to the barn. There, in the ground, were a set of boot prints.

"I was with Joel. We've dated off and on," Eleanor stated, emphasizing the off. "Those do kinda look like the prints his cowboy boots would leave behind."

"I don't know what the two of you are up to, but I would like for it to stop."

"I haven't seen him for over a week! He never even got out of the truck that first night I was here."

"Maybe, Eleanor, the real monsters are out there, trying to get in here."

"But if he was here, I knew nothing about it!"

"Is that the truth?"

"It is, Rick. I would never do something like this to make a story more than what it is."

"Good, because I was hoping no one was killing off horses for that reason. Because that person would be a real monster."

"I swear. Look, I gotta get to work. Mind if I stop by again later?"

"Okay," Rick said after a few moments thought. "And if I'm not here, go on and let yourself in."

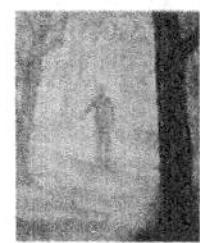

Even with Rick's peculiar and sometimes brusque personality, Eleanor couldn't stay away from the property's simple beauty. There was a compulsion to be there that brought her back that same evening. Luckily, Rick was gone when she arrived, and the place was hers to explore alone. She stood at the top of the pasture, taking in the view of the property as it sloped down to the canal. In the early evening breeze, the last of the summer's wildflowers danced. Lightning bugs dotted the air. She let herself in the farmhouse.

Inside, she returned to the line of family portraits that documented the generations of Turnbaughs who had called this place home. She flipped to a clean page in her notebook, but her thoughts trailed off to her awareness of the unease the portraits created in her. Above all else, she was shocked at the place of prominence given to the women over the men. Ladies first.

She lingered in the house longer than she'd planned. It was so easy to imagine herself here, with the luxury of it all, the security, and the freedom to live on her own, to write and not worry about covering rent and student loan payments. Rick's opaque offer was more than appealing. Perhaps it was more than the convenience of it all and having this place to herself. She was beginning to feel rooted in the land like no other place she'd ever been.

At that thought a shriek filled the air as it had that first night she visited the property. But this time, she had confidence on her side. She stormed outside toward the barn to stand between whatever it was and the horses. With Rick gone, she knew she was their only line of defense. Even she was surprised at how quickly her moods had turned, from bliss, to fear, to rage. It was almost as if she had become a mother of sorts to the place, wanting to protect what interest she had in it, even if that interest was still a dream. Because dreams, she knew, had to be protected, too.

Eleanor stood outside the barn and witnessed the pines moving to and fro. Something was coming. But she held her ground, planting her feet and squaring her shoulders at the approaching intruder. "Stay away!" she hollered.

At that, like a miracle, peace returned. The pasture stilled and became quiet.

A little more than a month had passed. Eleanor's first story about Rick's horse farm had gained enough attention to be turned into a four-part serial and had even led to requests for her to write additional human-interest pieces about the surrounding area. All the time together had changed most reservations Eleanor had about Rick. With each story, she spent more time at the farm interviewing him, and with each interview, the two of them gradually became more than partners in telling the story of his farm. They quickly became a couple on the precipice of a romantic interlude that neither would either admit or deny was happening.

"It's a harvest moon," she said, as they swayed together on the front porch glider, taking in the view down the open meadows to the canal.

"Perfect weather and lighting," he answered. "You'll love the glow of the autumn colors in the moonlight."

"You know, for as eerie as things on this property can be, I can't stay away."

"You're preaching to the choir, sister."

"How's your skin?"

"The cooler weather helps. I'm a big fan of autumn, and winter. I know, that makes me even odder." Rick smiled.

"Not at all." She sat beside him and ran her fingers along his hairline, allowing the shedding skin to litter the shrinking space between them. "I think it's romantic, actually. All the better to snuggle up."

"Well, if you're going to be stuck anywhere in a blizzard, there are worse places," he said. She moved in closer to him.

"Maybe you'll get lucky and that will happen," she said.

"That may take some getting used to."

Eleanor laughed bitterly at his remark and put some distance between them.

"I didn't mean it that way. It's not you — "

"Right, Rick. It's not me. It's you. You're the one with the issues, commitment, mommy, all that. It's not me. I'm just here keeping you company. And the story, well that even became second place to you, to what I thought was us."

"I like the story of us, Eleanor." He took her chin and lifted her head, leaning in close. "There hasn't been anyone who could accept me for what I am."

"If that bothered me, I'd have left after wrapping up the story." Eleanor stood to leave.

"Don't go!" he growled.

"Why not?"

"What I meant to say before ... it's not you. It's not me. Or this rash. There's just something else I haven't told you."

"Well when you're ready to talk, let me know. I'm out. Maybe you can pick at your own skin tonight."

A shriek echoed off the trees. Eleanor quickened her exit from the farm. As she moved, the tall grass and wilting wildflower stems roiled behind her. She hopped in her car as something latched on to the rear bumper, clawing at the ancient paint, scoring the sheet metal. Looking over to the passenger seat she saw Joel's bandana, and screamed. Her old sedan failed to turn over as the engine drowned. Her cries for help went unheard, and she looked up to the house as her only escape, her only chance at refuge. She whimpered as she ran back to the house.

Relief flooded her system as she threw open the door to the farmhouse and called for Rick. There was no answer. Her adrenaline surged. She didn't want to be alone in the house.

On the porch she heard leaden footsteps scuff along the decking. She moved through the house, switching on the lights in every room she passed through. She heard the horses begin to bray. She went to them, fearing for their safety, and seeking shelter in their company.

As she swung open the barn door, she was greeted by a childlike cry of someone missing their mother. A paint horse foal stood before her. Eleanor rubbed her eyes; she hadn't seen a foal in the barn before. Could it be?

The foal nuzzled her and walked toward the opening to the pasture, seeming to ask her to follow. That same piercing shriek filled her ears again, splitting them open, her eardrums feeling as though they were about to burst. She followed the foal, out to the pasture, and over to where Leddy had been murdered. The foal circled the area with ceremonial importance, pushing at the gate. The young horse seemed to understand that the ground had been hallowed by its mother's death.

A gentle rustle filled the empty darkness inside the pines. The twisted cedars inside their periphery stood guard against the moonlight, allowing only shadows to play inside. "Rick?" She called out. Another rustle in the trees. She felt something touch her shoulder and turned. Nothing. And then again, this time landing just above her breast. It was dark, sappy brown and tinged with red. Another shriek called out from the trees that caused her to look up. Joel's body fell through the branches and crashed at her feet. He'd been disemboweled. A note hung around his neck. "*I'd never leave you like he did.*"

Eleanor screamed and ran back to the house. Rick followed, dancing through the trees, pulling at the largest branches and pointing their bark-covered fingers at her. Another set of shrieks filled the night, causing her ears to ring again. As she made her way through the hall, she knocked a few of the family portraits to the floor. She took cover by the living room fireplace, beside the bay window offering her a clear view of the property.

"You can't run from me, Eleanor."

"Rick?"

"Yes, Eleanor, it's me. Look at the rash. It isn't a rash. It's the real me, under my skin."

"Stay back," she whimpered, trapped in the corner of the room.

"I won't hurt you," he said. "Weren't you looking for the Jersey Devil? You're looking at him."

"You killed Joel!" Anguish beat at Eleanor's heart. "And Leddy! How could you?"

"Yes, I did kill Joel. Leddy, well, she died in labor. And I needed to feed. I never would've harmed her, and I'm so glad you've met her foal. We are *kin*. But Joel, he was a different story."

"He never hurt anyone." Her eyes darted back and forth, minnows in fishbowls, seeking an escape.

"He was holding you back. That is a lifetime of hurt, Eleanor. And don't act like he was totally innocent. Do you know how many times I'd caught him poaching deer on this land? His time had come. Oh, Eleanor. I've known your Joel longer than you can imagine. And let me tell you this — there are more like him out there, who do nothing but take. It was time he gave something back." Her body convulsed as she watched Rick move closer to her. "Now, do you want the rest of the story?"

"But, we're too far from the Pine Barrens. You can't be ..."

"Please. Why stay there, where you simple-minded people are always looking? No, we've lived here for generations. I visit the Pine Barrens to keep up appearances."

Eleanor grabbed a fire poker and swung it madly. She watched as Rick ripped what remained of his shirt from his chest, fully exposing a plush layer of hair and graying skin.

She charged him. The poker pierced his left arm. He winced and turned into the weapon, using it as leverage to bring her down, and leveled it at her throat as she hit the floor. He stomped one hoof next to her head. Dust billowed up from between the old pine floorboards.

"You see, Eleanor, every thirteenth child in the family is born like me. Once we reach a certain age, the changes begin. You think I left the life I had to come back here? It's an amazing property, but there was nothing here for me. Or, as I should properly say, no one was here for me. My own parents feared what I would become. That is why my father was so protective of this place. Because of me and what people would do if they found out. He was guarding a secret — not all *this*."

She looked up at him. He picked her up and carried her to a chair commanding the view through the bay window. "This was Mother's chair. Do you like it?"

Eleanor shook her head. She asked, "But why have kids? Why keep it going on? Why not end this if it's so bad?"

"Being me isn't so bad. It's how people perceive me. I don't kill for fun. I kill to eat. Unlike guys like Joel who spend their autumns out there shooting deer for kicks. And don't you dare say you disagree with me. Because I know you better than you think."

Eleanor fidgeted in the chair.

"I chose you, because I knew you could be the one. And you proved that to me. You accepted me for what I was, for having that disgusting rash all over my body. True, you didn't know I was changing, but how I looked didn't faze you at all."

"If I knew you were a killer, I wouldn't have fallen like that. You're a monster."

"You're wrong. The world out there is the monster. All I wanted was to be left alone. The same holds true for each of those Turnbaughs on the wall. And you know what? It never happens. People come to hunt us down like we're some sort of trophy."

"You can't keep me here."

"No, I can't. And that's for the best, because I wouldn't want you here if you didn't want to stay."

"Then let me go. Please." She fidgeted some more. Tears filled her eyes.

"That's not the Eleanor I fell in love with. My Eleanor is a strong woman. So please, speak up. Speak your mind. Because becoming a Turnbaugh takes strength. Look at those women on the wall. None of them were weak."

She looked him up and down, at the hair covering his body, the hooves, and the claws that penetrated from beneath his former cuticles. She let him sift his claws through her hair, straightening tangles and combing out the pine needles that had become matted in her flowing blond strands. He caressed her back with the smooth, upper surfaces of his claws. With each stroke she felt him gingerly bring her closer to him.

"I can't," she said. "It's too much."

"I know how you feel about this place," he said. "You've fallen in love with it. And me, or more like the other me. But don't you worry. This look tonight, it's only a phase. I won't always look like *this*. But, that all hinges on one thing. You."

With waning strength, she pushed at his chest only to have her fingers become ensnared by the coarse hairs covering his body. Like tendrils of vines the hairs coupled themselves to her.

"Every story, Eleanor, has a beginning, a middle, and an end. You always come back because this place haunts your memories. You don't have to leave it again. It can be yours. I can't make you stay. But I won't let you go. And I don't want to have to do that."

"You wouldn't." Her eyes lit up.

"There's the woman I fell in love with. All that desire and rage. It's exactly what's needed to carry on this tradition. You have a choice that few people ever get, Eleanor. You know your beginning. It was a simple one. You could be up there on that wall, a matriarch who extended our lineage, a history that predates this country. All you have to do is decide one thing."

She looked at him and he turned to the window. The harvest moon had reached its apex. Its light glinted off the pines and wrapped the landscape in its luminescence. She hung on that moment, and as he shifted, a ray of moonlight cast a pallor glow over his face.

"Eleanor," he called to her, over his shoulder, and then turned to face her.

"Is this your middle, or is it your end?"

The Unspoiled Harmonious Wilderness

River Eno

Pine Barrens, New Jersey
2021

"Can you hear that?" Willa kicked a broken pine branch out of her way and off the covered trail. It was officially dusk. The part of day when all the brown and green foliage begins to blend together, making it difficult to judge distance or see tree roots protruding from the ground. "It sounds like a flute … but also a little different. It echoes. Can you hear it?"

"Of course, I can hear it," mumbled Francine.

"They were playing Eugène Oneguine in the museum this morning. This is similar … maybe just in the sadness of it. It's beautiful though." Willa looked around and up at the trees. "I wonder where it's coming from."

Francine shrugged, her mood no better for the questions.

Willa continued behind, but slowly. She fiddled with the scarf around her neck. It was freezing, unlike the last few disturbingly warm Novembers. And after fifteen more minutes of crickets and cracking branches, she finally lost patience with Francine's mopey silence.

"This is stupid. You're not talking or singing or anything! I feel like we're funeral marching through this forest. What is the point of us being here if you're so unhappy about it?"

"If you want to go, then go. I didn't force you to come."

"No, you didn't force me, but I felt like I had to, if only so you don't get lost out here all by yourself."

"Please. I know the way, Willa. I can do it in my sleep."

"But doing this doesn't make you happy. And if it doesn't make you happy, we don't have to do it just because it was our yearly ritual with Mom." Willa's boot hit an upended rock and she stumbled.

"So, we just forget her altogether!" Francine argued. "The way you do the rest of the year."

"What the hell, Francine! That isn't what I meant, and you know it. How could you even suggest that I've forgotten Mom?"

Francine used a small machete to clear the thinner pine limbs out of their way. She stayed quiet; she knew she'd gone too far.

"Wait, stop. There's something in my shoe." Willa

leaned her hand against the nearest tree and pulled off her hiking boot. "Not a day goes by that I don't think about Mom. I loved her as much as you. But I don't let it take me over."

"What does that mean?"

"You're overwhelmed with grief and you stress because of it."

"I'm not obsessed!"

"I didn't say obsessed, but you have always had those tendencies, and when Mom died, they kicked into overdrive."

"Like how?"

Willa huffed. "You eat the same foods at the same time every single day. You go to the gym on Mondays, Wednesdays and Fridays. Tuesdays are for the supermarket and Thursdays are work catch-up days. Saturdays you clean regardless if your apartment is dirty or not and Sundays are for laundry and mopping. You do things because you can't stop yourself. Even if it's detrimental."

"I'm particular, not obsessed!" Francine stomped her foot on the ground, creating only a thud against the dense bed of pine needles and broken branches.

"Right, whatever." Willa dropped her boot to the ground and jammed her foot back into it, searching for patience. She wanted to support her sister, she really did, but her attitude made it almost impossible.

"I just need to do this, Willa." Francine began walking, a bit quicker this time. "Can you understand that?"

"Yes, I can. But we keep coming here, rattling through these woods, and you're not smiling. You're not talking. This isn't fun. And this isn't honoring her memory ... it's wallowing in grief and self-pity."

The sisters continued until dark had fallen and they came upon the old cemetery. Willa enjoyed it; cemeteries calmed her nerves, and the racing water in the creek nearby soothed her head. She knew Francine didn't like it. The dead left her feeling lonely, and the sound of the creek always made her shiver in the chill.

They stopped at the biggest monument, same place every time. They sat on the wide concrete gate surrounding it, resting from the longest portion of their journey. Willa took a long breath and searched her rucksack for protein bars. She hoped the day Francine overcame the feelings of abandonment their mother's death had caused came sooner than later. She didn't know how much more she could take. She felt it too, she just tried really hard not to let it get to her.

Francine riffled through her pack and pulled out a flashlight. She took out a second pair of gloves and put the dirty ones in a cloth laundry bag next to the machete at the bottom of her pack.

"Come on, let's get this done." Willa picked at Francine's shirt sleeve and smiled. She handed her sister one of her favorite fruit and nut bars. "Maybe we'll see the Jersey Devil this time."

Francine smiled, though not really wanting to. She took the bar and slung her rucksack on her back. She flipped the flashlight on, and they headed through the cemetery toward the same small clearing that marked the end of their designated trail.

"I think this thing needs batteries." Francine banged the head of the flashlight against her palm, to force the dim light brighter. "It's so dark. And it's freezing out here!"

"Well, you knew I had to work, Francy. So you knew we'd be starting late. I'm still pretty far down the museum totem pole as far as time off is concerned."

"I didn't mean it like that!" Maybe it was the use of an old nickname, or maybe Francine was getting tired, and a little bored of this trail too. "I wasn't complaining. I'm sorry."

"Oh," Willa said, surprised. "Okay."

The darkness closed in on the forest, and for a while the sisters hiked in silence, wading through the woods with a practiced skill that showed they had traversed the same path many times before. Neither was particularly afraid of the forest at night, but their thoughts combined with the bitter chill put hesitation in both their steps.

Distant sounds of a flute echoed softly around them.

"Do you remember cousin Jared's twenty-fifth birthday party?" Willa asked. "At that restaurant with all the games? And Scott was playing a perfect game of shuffleboard, and I grab—"

"You grabbed his last ball and threw it up the alley," Francine said accusingly. "And it landed right in the zero hole!"

"He was so angry." Willa laughed.

"Of course, he was," Francine agreed. "Aunt Maddy and Mom got into a big fight that night, because you lied and said Scott said you could take the last ball."

Willa almost had to stop walking she was laughing so hard.

"It turned the whole night from family fun to family feud."

"So what." Willa shrugged and frowned at Francine's sanctimonious attitude. "We were kids, and Scott was a jerk half the time anyway."

"It was still wrong of you to lie."

Willa's eyes rolled so far back she nearly lost her balance.

"Anyway, do you remember the story Uncle Chase told that night about the Jersey Devil?"

"Not really." Francine shrugged.

"It was like the ones Mom would sometimes tell when we hiked." Willa poked Francine's back with a stick she kicked and picked up on the trail. "A dark and quiet night in the Barrens, someone hears something strange, and the Devil pops out of the shadows and everyone runs away."

"I guess, yeah. So?"

"Everyone is afraid of the Jersey Devil, but I don't think it's ever hurt anything."

"Livestock," Francine said. "It's always eating livestock from the local farmers in those stories."

"I meant a person. There's no story of it ever hurting a person, is there?"

"No." Francine shook her head. "I don't think so."

At the edge of the meadow that marked the end of their journey, Francine suddenly stopped short, bringing Willa into her back.

"What the hell, Francy!"

"Shh!" Francine lowered her voice to a whisper. "There's a bear asleep in the clearing."

"What?" Willa whispered. "Where? Are you sure?"

Francine pointed the flashlight beam close to a dark heap ahead of them. Willa watched the mound rise and then fall with the slow rhythm of a sleeping animal.

"Shit," Willa breathed in her sister's ear. Black bears were making a comeback, but she'd never seen hide nor hair of one. Willa slowly cupped her hand over Francine's ear. "Did you bring bear mace?"

"No." Francine swallowed nervously. "Did you?"

"Why would I ask you if I had!" Willa whispered back.

Very slowly, Francine moved her right leg back, allowing Willa time to realize what she wanted to do. They each quietly lowered their feet to solid ground and then did the same with the left foot.

Francine kept the flashlight near the sleeping heap. The light was dancing because she was trembling, so she shifted her finger slowly to shut the light, when suddenly the animal lifted its large head off the ground, half turned and looked at them with the glowing eyes of a dragon.

The head was attached to a long neck that kept rising. Francine raised the flashlight, shining the hazy, shaking light onto the creature as it pushed itself up on long hind legs and then its hooved feet. It was at least ten feet tall. It had horns, and Willa managed to grip her sister and whisper the only thing that came to her mind.

"That is not a bear."

Francine shook her head and then nodded, too afraid to remember how to respond. The beast reached its smaller arms outward as if grabbing or stretching. The sharp talons on the end of its large, strange paws clacked together. They watched as one wing moved slowly out and then the other grew to mirror it. A wave traveled along its back, rippling down the wings to the edges.

The three of them stood there, still and quiet, for a few heartbeats. Francine and Willa took in the sight of the infamous Jersey Devil from the glow of the flashlight. And they wondered, what in the name of the Devil was it going to do with them?

The creature reared up, made a screeching cry, and pounded its hooves onto the sandy ground. Francine fumbled and dropped the flashlight and the sisters grabbed at each other. They crouched and squeezed their eyes shut. Maybe they were wrong about the Devil only eating livestock, and they were going to die at the hands of an urban legend, a folk tale!

The Devil stomped and screeched again. But it didn't move any closer, and after a moment, Willa peeked open an eye. The creature lowered its head, blew a deep grunting breath out its nostrils and cocked its head to the side.

"What's it doing?" Willa whispered.

"Shh," Francine whispered back.

"Don't shush me." Willa pushed her sister. "Just look at it."

Francine opened her eyes slowly, and the creature clomped one hoof and jangled its head. The long, elk-like horns swayed awkwardly.

"It's like it's trying to communicate or something." Willa rose up a bit.

The beast blew another gust of air and then lowered its head. Willa stood slowly. The creature clacked its claws, and she froze.

"Why did you stand! Why would you do that?" Francine grabbed her sister's belt loop to pull her down.

"Because we can't just stay crouched to the ground! It's not moving any closer. Maybe we can run." Willa took a tentative step backwards.

"Don't!" Francine used her sister's arm to pull herself up.

The Devil backed up and grunted. But then it came forward, only slowly, almost timidly. It lowered its head, and Willa nervously reached out to touch its downturned chin.

"Be careful, ladies!"

"Shit!" Francine and Willa yelled, grabbing each other's hands.

They spun around. A man was behind them. At least it was a man's voice coming from the vague outline of a person in the darkness. Francine's flashlight was in the dirt, so it was difficult to see. The man wasn't too close, but they were between him and the Devil. Not an ideal place to be.

"My apologies. My intention was to warn you, not frighten you." His accent was strange and old, something neither of them had heard before. "He has been here too long, and he is ... how is the word? Grumpy?"

Francine and Willa stood in the dark, cold and mystified. They tried desperately to see better. To make sense of the scene playing out before them.

"Who ... who are you?" stuttered Francine.

The man took a step closer, and it was suddenly a bit brighter around him than it had been the moment before, as if his own internal light radiated from him like a firefly. He was at least six feet tall. He had wide, intense eyes and longish, dark, curly hair half covering pointed ears. A long, curly goatee, the hair of which grew up the sides of his jaw and into his hairline. His face was slightly elongated, and he was overtly handsome. He had horns, the same type of elk-like horns as the Devil, only smaller. The sisters stepped back, putting them closer to the beast. The man took another step toward them, becoming brighter still.

"Again, my apologies for my abruptness." His beautiful accent turned his words into a melody.

"Oh my," whispered Willa, staring at the unique stranger. His feral appearance looked familiar, like so many paintings in the Classics section at the museum. "You um ..."

"You're not wearing clothes," Francine finished her

sister's words on a nervous breath, her eyes wandering down his body. The stranger had a line of curly hair down the middle of his broad chest leading to generous genitalia. The same hair covered his thighs and traveled down his legs. "Oh," said Francine, the pitch of her voice heightening, "you have hooves too."

"I do," said the stranger with a small, but wild smile. "And, I do not own clothing. As a satyr, I have never had the need."

"Oh, well sure," said Willa, feeling like she was losing the ground under her feet. "Of course not. Why would a satyr need clothes?"

Francine noticed something in the stranger's hand. "What are you holding?" she demanded, albeit cautiously.

"This?" The stranger lifted his hand. His fingernails were dirty. "Pipes for music. A flute, if you will. I was just over there," he pointed into the trees across the clearing, "by the creek, restringing and testing them, when I heard voices."

Francine and Willa looked at each other, understanding now where the music they'd heard all day was coming from. And in that moment, Willa realized who the stranger was. Only, the idea made absolutely no sense. Of course, nothing at the moment made sense.

"Would you like to see it?" He stretched his arm and in his glowing hand were eight hollowed reeds cut to different sizes and strung together with twine. When neither sister took the instrument, the satyr put the pipes to his lips and played a short, pleasant tune. The low, dulcet tones filled the air, settling onto their skin and bathing their bodies in a pleasing warmth that radiated around them like the heat of the sun on a clear spring day. Both sisters relaxed, and they smiled.

"Enchanting," said Willa.

A sudden loud thumping made them jump, bringing their attention back to the Devil they'd carelessly forgotten behind them.

"Dammit," Francine snapped, and she turned quickly back to the stranger, not wanting him out of sight either. "Who are you?" Uncertainty gave her the boost of bravery she was looking for earlier.

"Who am I?" The satyr smiled and gestured to the Devil. "I am his father."

"What? His father?" Francine scowled at the stranger.

"How exactly?" asked Willa tentatively.

"Sit." The stranger gestured to the damp ground, thick with years of collected pine needles and deadfall. "And I will tell you a story."

New Jersey – 1735

The farmhouse was deep in the Barrens, set inside a large, man-made clearing. It was a stone structure with two fireplaces. One in the front parlor and one in the large, working kitchen. The house had looked old when it was built, typical of the time, but it was formidable, made by skilled hands. But it wasn't the house that caught the attention of Pan. It was the chaos. Twelve children had been born there. All in the front bedroom. And there was noise. Glorious noise. The young ones played and laughed and cried and panicked. They conversed and told secrets. They loved and shared moments of life, and they grew as humans are wont to do.

Truth be told, Pan was visiting the wilderness of the Americas long before Mother's thirteenth child. The land was untamed, uncultivated and feral — like him. He too had twelve sons and could barely resist the calling of the twelve in the place they called New Jersey, no matter how far it was from his home. Mountains were mountains. Wilderness was wilderness. Sex and chaos were everywhere. Pan was as comfortable there as he was roaming his home of Arcadia.

It was a blindingly hot day as Mother harvested her garden collecting tomatoes and strawberries. It was difficult to grow what she needed in the Pine Barrens sand, but she managed. And what she couldn't grow herself, she would trade, using the fruits she produced and the beautiful Gentiana and Narthecium that grew abundantly behind the root cellar.

She was pregnant with her thirteenth child and between the sun's heat and glare, and the extra weight of a belly full of babe, she was exhausted and had little patience. She straightened to her knees, leaned the basket of overripe strawberries beside her and ran a hand over the thin, homemade, cotton dress covering her swollen tummy. For so long she had wished, desperately, that it was flat and empty, a state she had seldom known over the last twenty years. Those thoughts filled her with guilt each time the babe moved or when one of the young ones voiced their excitement for the coming child.

Today, however, like the two days before, the babe lay quiet and still in her womb, a thing that had never happened to her before. She had heard stories from other women, and she couldn't decide if she would be devastated if the babe were to be stillborn or elated.

Mother gently shook her belly with her hands, something she did in the past to keep the sleeping babe awake and on a better schedule when born. Those times, the babe would kick and move. Now, nothing.

Mother sighed, particularly worn, but she needed to get the fruit ready for the week's end market. She'd had the eldest take the young ones into the woods to collect acorns for flour so she could gather the last of the fruit unhindered. But she was having a difficult time concentrating. Her legs began to cramp, as well as her abdomen, and as quickly as her extra weight would allow, she stood. The basket of berries tipped, and she stepped in them when catching her balance.

When she saw she had ruined the harvest, tears sprang to her eyes. Standing there, sweat dripping down her spine, unable to move her foot out of the crushed fruit, a strange and cataclysmic calm washed over her, as if watching a tree fall knowing you cannot get out of its way.

Mother stared at the ground. Her face ashen. Her expression trancelike.

Then suddenly she fell to her knees and shrieked a pain she had never heard before — even during childbirth. The sound was filled with a lifetime's worth of strife, oppression and a multitude of emotions there were no words for. Mother shrieked until she had no voice left. And then she fell over into the berries.

Pan was sitting with his back against a pitch pine, his favorite tree in the Barrens, creating a new song on his flute. His ears perked and twisted at the screaming coming from the way of the house in the clearing — the house with the twelve children. He smiled and dashed in the direction of the noise. But what he found flattened his happiness. Mother was on the ground, hunched over. She was surrounded by four of her younger children. They were leaning over her, calling her name, crying.

Pan walked among them. His powerful, yet concealed presence shifted them back until he had a better view. Mother's eyes were closed. Her mouth was open, as though her last thought passed her lips before she fell unconscious. Pan watched her. He looked at her legs. There was some blood, but no babe. He felt ... sorrow. He was used to her presence and did not like thinking she was going to die. His brow furrowed and he blew a hard breath through his nostrils.

The children huddled silently. The oldest in the group left to find Father. Pan knelt, his hand hovered over her person, wondering what he should do. He did not like being in this position, so uncertain of his actions.

Mother's hand was half lying on her protruding belly, and Pan listened, finally realizing the void emanating from the womb. It was still but full, yet it was empty. He assumed this was the cause of Mother's condition, the pain he saw frozen on her face. He touched her shoulder, gently pressing until she rolled to her back. The children yelped and moved farther away.

Pan's fingers moved carefully, reverently, over Mother's face, her full breasts and belly, barely rising with her ever slowing breath. She did not smell well. Finally, with much reservation, but much more curiosity, he rested his hand upon her body.

Pan's magik flared—the human was a dark hole his energy could fill—but he pulled it back, and instead listened. The motionless being inside Mother had been that way for two suns. Pan stared at Mother. The thing that made her who she was, was fading too, nearly gone. He sighed. Unlike most humans, he cared for

Mother. Since she had arrived, he was in awe of her strength and marveled at her knowledge of the old ways, although her husband thought her superstitious. He found himself proud of her determination and skill. Many days he'd sit by her as she labored at the shallow end of the river. He would play his music and watch her moods play out in her large, dark brown eyes. So expressive they were. A story told with every glance.

He could fix her; she was not entirely gone. He could give her back life, if he desired ... if that was what she desired. And although the babe in her womb would pose a challenge, it was small, and he was sure he could fix it, with a bit of determination.

He tried to listen to her thoughts. Only there was nothing but space and calm. No words or chaos, which was unfortunate as he was fluent in chaos. He was uncertain again and then he thought, she is female, and all females would surely be devastated at the loss of a babe. Had he not been drawn to the hysteria of other females in similar situations?

With more certainty, Pan rested his hand on Mother's belly until an indentation appeared, scaring her terrified offspring even more. His palm and fingers grew warm as his energy seeped deep into Mother's body and womb. The vitality invigorated Mother's blood and then, combining his fortitude with hers, Pan reshaped the dead form in her body to something fresh and beautiful; his ideas became a mental canvas that created and breathed robust life into the motionless carcass until it suddenly twitched and kicked inside of her. Mother's body finally stirred, and she took a deep breath. Pan smiled, pleased with his effort.

Slowly Mother opened her eyes, her expression soft, but confused, and then she winced. Her hand gripped the heavy, foreign flutter in her belly. Panic filled her widening eyes as she focused on Pan above her, his magik opening her human sight to all the preternatural wonders around her; if only for a short while.

Pan meant to leave but became curious when her anger turned. Her brows furrowed and her forehead creased with the pain of life.

"You," she whispered weakly. "I think I know you ..."

Pan smiled. He knew there were times she felt him, even saw him, beside her. He knew she was special.

"Why?" Mother asked. "Why do this to me?"

Pan's smile faded. What did she mean? She was dying, and he had saved her. He had saved her babe! His large hand hovered over hers.

Mother's tears flowed fast, but her voice remained low and saddened with grief.

"I was at peace ... finally ... at peace. You have cursed me." Mother clutched at her dirty dress with both hands and widened her eyes at Pan. "He has cursed me!"

Pan backed away as her children began to gather. He watched as Father and three more offspring ran into the field with the wheelbarrow and armfuls of bed linens.

"You have cursed me!" Mother continued to cry.

Perplexed, Pan fled into the forest until he was concealed completely by the heavy boughs of pine.

Mother lay tied to the bed, her arms stretched out toward the posts. Father thought it prudent considering she would not stop beating at her belly and trying to push the babe out before it was due. She was now in a moment of peace, her voice resting from the screams she could not control during each contraction.

It had been almost three weeks since she was found in the field, bleeding and hysterical. The babe had taken its time to join the outside world. Until this afternoon.

Another contraction began. The muscles in Mother's belly tightened, and her legs pulled close to her body. She moaned and grunted, bloody fluid leaking from between her legs. Another high-pitched wail escaped from deep in her chest.

The old midwife, Mrs. Abbett, was excellent at herbs, delivering hundreds of healthy babes in her time. But this one seemed different. Wrong somehow. The movement against the belly was not natural. She tried not to let Mother's ramblings of gods and monsters affect her judgement, but the skin was more swollen and harder than ever she'd seen a laboring belly, and she was sure she had seen what must have been the babe's hand, only ... it did not quite look like a hand.

No sooner did the midwife think she herself could take no more of the wailing when Mother quieted and fell back onto the bed, unconscious. Her legs fell open and her belly rippled and bulged. In the candlelight silence, Mrs. Abbett saw two claws reach out. Small, but strong. The pointy nails groped and then latched onto Mother's thighs and pulled.

The old midwife grabbed the small cross around her neck and backed to the wall. She knocked into the small table she used for her supplies, and the basin rocked off and smashed against the hard wood floor. She watched, unblinking, barely breathing, as the elbows emerged and bent, pulling against mother's skin even harder. Finally, a small, deer-like head popped out, its long jaw opening and closing, seeming to gasp for air, looking like an ancient dragon. It hooked its short claws into the bed sheet and dragged the rest of itself from Mother, plopping onto the blood-soaked bed.

Mrs. Abbett, now at the far wall, by the wardrobe, shook uncontrollably. Father knocked hard on the door. He wanted to see his wife and new child. Only the old midwife couldn't move.

"... the Lord is my shepherd; I shall not want. He maketh me lie down in green pastures; he leadeth me beside still waters — oh dear god!" The woman cried and sank further into the corner when the child began to move about.

It shook itself weakly, like a wet animal. Its wings peeled from its saturated body and extended awkwardly to catch its balance. The midwife saw small, nubby horns on its head and the spidering ridges of bone on the wings protruding from its back. It teetered on small ... hooves! The creature had a long tail it swished this way and that! The old woman lost her breath. Her eyes rolled back into her head, and she slid down the wardrobe, landing in an unconscious heap in the corner.

The little creature flapped its wings, becoming a bit steadier as it learned its weight and blood began to flow steadily into its legs. It plodded around the end of the bed until Mother made a small pitiful noise.

"Husband," she breathed, nearly too weak to speak.

The creature sniffed the air in her direction and flapped its wings in an effort to assist its wobbling legs. It clambered over Mother's body toward her head. It examined Mother's face, pushing its snout against her shoulder.

"Demon." Mother breathed the word on the last breath she'd ever take.

The heavy bedroom door swung open and banged against the wall. The startled creature jumped and teetered and flapped its wings. There was yelling and screaming. The creature stretched its wings full and leapt over Mother. It half flew, half scrambled across the bed. Finally gaining flight, it flew into the window, smashing through and flying out into the dark night.

"Oh my goodness," said Willa, wiping the tears from her eyes. "That was awful."

"It was," said the satyr. "Although, it is, as humans say, history."

The Jersey Devil grunted and shrieked, flapping its wings, creating a gust of wind that traveled fiercely through the clearing. Francine and Willa were still on the ground, hunched over and covering their ears to shield them from the ear-splitting pitch of the Devil's cry.

"I realize it is a difficult memory for you," yelled the satyr over the beast's outburst. "However, I need you to control yourself. Am I understood?"

The Devil pulled its wings to its back and grunted. It blew a loud breath and flumped back on its haunches, seeming to brood from the scolding, which made the sisters feel uneasy and yet somehow mournful.

"Yes," said Francine, "it is sad. I'm not sure what to say." She frowned, both supernatural creatures were so difficult to comprehend. Even with them standing in front of her. And all she could think of was the end of the story, when the Devil crawled to his mother ... and she died. Francine turned her head and wiped the tears streaming down her face. "And so, you're Pan in this story?" she asked, clearing her throat. "You're the Greek god?"

"I am saying that, yes." The handsome, softly glowing satyr stood, smiled and bowed. "I am god of the forest and of the woodland creatures ... and of lustful behavior." He smiled wider and shamelessly.

"This is all so fantastical," said Francine.

Willa was thinking, and she was getting nervous. She knew enough about Pan from her studies to know he wasn't always the friendliest god. None of the ancient gods she'd read about seemed all that friendly.

"How are we seeing you?" asked Willa cautiously. "I heard that we..."

Pan stared at Willa, allowing a few moments to pass. "Humans?" the god finished for her.

"Yes ... we humans, couldn't look at your true face without..."

"Losing your minds?" The god smiled.

Willa swallowed and nodded.

"What do you mean?" Francine looked at Willa, alarmed. "That's a thing that could happen? Losing our minds because we looked at him?"

"You will not," said the god. "In this arena..." he held his arms wide, insinuating the entire clearing, "I have control of what you see and how you see it."

"So, the way you look now," said Willa suspiciously, "isn't your true face?"

"Let us say," Pan's dark eyes blazed, "it is one of them."

That wasn't exactly reassuring to the sisters. And as stubborn as Francine could be, she felt she was going to have to believe in all of this sooner rather than later. If only so she could keep her sister safe from the god with many faces.

"Why do you want us to see you at all?" Willa asked, knowing of stories between gods and humans that didn't end so well for the human.

"I do not know for certain," said Pan, and he narrowed his brows in thought. "I am thinking I may like the two of you."

"The way you liked Mother?" asked Willa, without thought.

"And why..." Francine stepped on her sister's question and pointed to the Devil. "Why didn't it eat us when we first got here?"

The creature cried out, and the sisters covered their ears once again.

"My God!" cried Francine when quiet returned to the meadow.

"Can you blame him!" said the Greek god sternly. "You were insulting!"

"Insulting," repeated Willa.

"Firstly, he is a he, not an it. And have you ever heard one tale of the Jersey Devil, of my Devil, hurting or killing a human?" Pan's brows rose high.

"We were actually talking about that earlier," said Willa. "No, I guess not."

"You guess not?" The god tsked at her, turned and gave the Devil a smile. "He has always been a good lad, in spite of his obvious differences."

"He's a he, huh?" said Willa and smiled at him. "Does he have a name?"

"He does," answered Pan.

"Maybe he hasn't eaten people," interrupted Francine, feeling scolded. "But he has frightened people and eaten a lot of livestock from the farms around here."

"Farmers should not be caging animals," said the god angrily. "No one should own any species of animal. And they should not be contained, for any reason. I do not like it. I am sure you would not like it."

"No," said Francine. "I wouldn't. But he still eats them."

"For some of us," Pan sighed, "... food is food. A child must eat! But that has no bearing on animals being caged!"

The sisters' eyes widened at hitting a nerve in the god's morals.

"Okay. Fair enough." Francine nodded, not wanting to anger the god with lots of faces, of which at least one could make them go crazy.

"Maybe we should talk about something besides the Devil's eating habits," said Willa.

"Can I ask you a question ..." Francine hesitated, wanting to address the god respectfully. She felt it probably wasn't appropriate to call him Pan, but she didn't know if she should say sir or god or sir god.

"Are questions not what you have been already asking?" Pan half smiled, and Francine was struck again by how handsome he was, and she wondered, if he was, in fact, keeping them from seeing his true appearance, was he doing something to make them think he was handsome? Pan's smile grew wider and less lopsided. "Ask away."

"If the Devil, or rather, your son, lives here, why don't people run into him all the time?"

"He does not live here. He has always stepped between two worlds. I knew it would be difficult for him to interact with the creatures on this plane." Pan sighed. "You are all so judgmental. And although he does love to be here, he gets agitated when humans are frightened by him and then come with torches and ropes and bags to kill him and put him on display."

"He is scary," said Francine defensively, looking at him sitting in the dark, waiting for his father to tell him what to do. "Well, not this minute he isn't."

Willa took a breath and started for where the Devil sat. Francine half-heartedly pulled her arm to stop her, because although she wasn't afraid the way she was before, she felt getting too close to either legend was probably a bad thing.

"He is a bit scary," said Willa. "But sort of sweet too." The creature watched Willa, cautious of the human's closeness. "Can I touch you, big guy?" Willa smiled up at him and noticed the stars teeming in the dark, night sky. "Strange, but it seems warmer and brighter somehow. I can see so clearly now."

"You are welcome," answered Pan.

Willa glanced at the satyr god, then back to the Devil. She reached up to the docile creature in front of her, elated when he reached his small arms down. She timidly touched his sharp nails and laughed nervously when he made grunting sounds and clacking noises with his claws. The Devil leaned forward, giving Willa pause, but she heard him inhale, sniffing … and then he blew out a hard breath, spraying her with Jersey Devil snot. Francine laughed and Willa grimaced, wiping away the wetness with her scarf.

It wasn't lost on Francine that though she was the one who persisted with this yearly ritual through the Barrens, it was Willa who always got so much more out of it. Even now, in the face of the unimaginable, it was Willa who was embracing it, much like their mother would have done. Willa was the one who could reminisce about her without anxiety and panic. So often Francine felt overwhelmed by her life, a fear she wasn't living it to its fullest, but she needed to keep on track. Their mother had passed away without warning, with so many things left undone, and Francine didn't want to leave her life unfinished. But as she watched Willa with the Devil, she felt, not for the first time, that her obsessions might be making her miss some really important things.

Pan stared at Francine. The god smiled, the corners of his mouth turning up into an almost wicked expression, and she took a step back.

"Death is not the end of all things," he said.

"Excuse me?" Francine frowned.

"Death is not final. It is merely one type of energy turning into another type of energy."

"It seems pretty final to us." Francine said sullenly.

"But you know now, things are rarely what they seem?" Pan gestured to the Devil and then he motioned for Francine to come closer.

Francine took a step forward and Pan opened his hand, palm up, fingers separated, as if he were holding an invisible ball. Very slowly, a bit of golden light appeared in the center. It swirled, blossoming into a spiral of colors — dark yellow, magenta, and blues and greens. Dozens, if not hundreds of small pinpricks of light appeared, floating around the dusty spiral like stars.

"It's beautiful." Francine stepped closer to see more clearly. "It looks like the Milky Way. What is it?"

"Energy," said Pan, smiling.

"Where did it come from?"

"Here. There." The god motioned with his free hand to the air around them and to the dark sky above. "Below. Everywhere."

The tiny stars, some brighter and bigger and some small but twinkling, moved slowly within the hand-held galaxy.

"That's amazing."

"I agree," said Pan and then he closed his fist and brushed his hands together. The gas and stars dissipated like dust in the wind.

"Oh," said Francine. "Where did it go?"

"Up there." The god pointed to the night sky. The same cluster was hovering a few feet over Francine's head and then it was gone as if someone blew away sand. "Energy cannot die. It merely moves from one place to the other."

"But," Francine whispered with tears in her eyes, "it isn't here anymore. I can't see its beauty."

"Why should you be the only one privy to beautiful things?"

Francine looked at the god with a gaping mouth.

"Francine, come here," Willa called.

Pan smiled. He motioned for Francine to go, and he lounged on the ground in the middle of the meadow and played a soft, relaxing song on his pipes.

"Come here, come here." Willa pulled Francine by her arm over to the Devil. "Watch this." Willa threw a pine branch up in the air and the Devil batted it with the back side of his wing, sending it flying into the trees. Willa threw a few more branches and each time the Devil knocked it into or over the tall pines.

Willa turned a wide, open smile to Francine. "He'd be great at baseball!"

The beast stepped behind Willa's back and nudged her off balance with his large head. She yelped and stumbled into Francine, and they landed in a heap on the grass. The Devil flapped his wings until he was above the trees and out of sight.

"You better run," yelled Willa, laughing.

"That's the strangest thing that's ever happened to me." Francine laughed, picking herself up off the ground, rubbing her backside. "And I think maybe I broke my hip."

"I'm pretty sure all of this is the strangest thing that will ever happen to us," Willa said.

The Devil landed on the other side of the clearing, and Willa rushed over to him.

"Do you think maybe we could," Willa looked at the Devil with a gleam in her eyes, "get a ride?"

The Devil flapped his wings and screeched into the quiet night. The sisters held their ears, unsure if that was an enthusiastic yes or a definite no.

"I am sorry to interrupt," interjected Pan, startling the sisters. His music had filled the area with the calming influence they felt when he played earlier, and they had actually forgotten he was there.

"As wonderful as all this has been. And believe me when I tell you it has been wonderful." The god winked at both women with a sensual shine in his eyes and an unabashed smile on his full lips. "The night has waned. Morning is near, and it is time for us to go."

"But," said Willa, "we've only just started."

"Please," begged Francine, feeling light of spirit for the first time in a long while. "Can't we have a few more minutes?"

"We have conversed, and we have all learned about the other. It is now time to depart." The Devil flapped his wings, but the god motioned for him to be quiet. "And we are already late."

The Devil lifted himself into the air, landing across the clearing behind his father.

"Will we ever see you again?" Willa asked excitedly, before realizing that seeing them again, especially Pan, the god with many wild faces, might not be something that was in the best interest of her and her sister. And maybe by now he'd realized he couldn't let them walk away after all they'd seen. Would he make them look at his terrible face, so they were literally incapable of telling what happened? Willa thought of the horrid story of Prometheus, who wasn't human, but was punished eternally for helping the ancient people.

Pan stared at Willa, in that way of his, as if he could hear the thoughts of anyone he set his eyes upon. The otherworldliness sharpened the lines of his face.

"I would hate for these woods to be trampled by a new set of gawking humans, hoping to find the Devil and now his father, the ancient, Greek god.

Even fantastical stories have a way of spreading, do they not?"

"We would never tell anyone we saw you here." Willa's mouth was dry as a bone.

Francine felt the chill begin to return to the clearing and her fears along with it. She immediately went to her sister's side and put her arm around Willa's shoulders.

"She's right. We won't say anything to anyone. Not a soul. Who would even believe us?"

"I know you will not." The god's voice was deeper than it had been all night.

Francine and Willa began to take steps away from him and his son.

"Stop." Pan commanded, and they did, because their feet wouldn't move them any farther. Pan cocked his head to the side. "How about we make an agreement. A pact."

"Okay," said Francine, too quickly.

"Wait," said Willa. "I'm not sure making deals with gods is the right thing to do."

"Depends on the deal." Pan smiled. "How could I harm you? My son is so happy." Pan took a breath and clasped his hands behind his back. He paced, thinking.

Francine and Willa thought the Devil looked as if he were smiling at them, and they smiled back, only anxiously.

"I propose we meet here. Twice a year. Once in late winter, at Lupercalia. And once in the autumn, at Mabon."

"Lupercalia?" asked Willa.

"Mabon?" asked Francine.

Pan frowned. "I suppose I can forgive you for not knowing of Lupercalia. The holiday celebrated in late winter ... in my honor." Pan's fingertips pressed his chest.

"Sorry." Willa squished up her nose apologetically. "So, by late winter ... you mean early March?"

"Let us say mid-February," Pan corrected.

"And Mabon?" asked Francine again.

Now Pan sighed. "I must say, both of you not knowing of Mabon, the second harvest at the autumnal equinox, is a bit shameful. What do humans celebrate if not the cycles of the Mother?"

"Thanksgiving." Willa shrugged. "Easter."

"What is Thanksgiving?"

"Okay," said Francine. "When is the autumn equinox?"

Willa shrugged again.

"In autumn," replied Pan, annoyed.

Francine huffed. "So, we'll meet you here around the middle of October?"

"How about the end of September?" Pan forced a smile.

"Okay, so the middle of February and the end of September?"

"Agreed." The god nodded.

"No wait, what days?" asked Willa

"In the middle," said Pan pointedly. "And at the end."

"Any day in the middle of February and any day at the end of September, and you'll just be here?"

"We will be here when you both arrive. I give you my word."

"And ... now we can leave?" Francine asked cautiously. "You trust that we won't say anything?"

"No, I do not trust that."

"But wait?" Francine said. "You said—"

"I like you both. However, I do not trust humans to keep secrets. It is not in their nature to do so. But it is no matter, because you will not remember me or my son or any of this."

The sisters swallowed.

Pan walked toward them, and they backed away. "I cannot touch you if you walk away from me."

"You want to touch us?" Francine stepped in front of Willow. "Touch how? Touch where? Touch why?"

"A simple touch," Pan said. "And our deal is done."

Francine pulled Willa farther back.

"If I do not touch you, then you cannot leave." The tone in the god's voice became blatantly serious. "If you cannot leave, we cannot leave, and we are already late. And we can be late no more."

The sisters looked at each other, afraid that the god might do something nefarious, and yet not as afraid as they were for the last few years. The pain of losing their mother influenced so much of their lives. And the wonder and freedom of this night made the shadow of that pain come into focus and dissipate at the same time. They could be forever afraid, or they could take a chance and see where it led. And if it didn't turn out exactly as they'd hoped, they'd deal with it then. Mother always said, things work out in unexpected ways. More than ever, they hoped that were true.

"I think it's okay, Francy." Willa took her sister's hand. "We're together. We'll be okay."

Francine nodded and Pan stepped slowly toward them. His heat and inner light intensified the closer he came. They could see his face clearly now. He was so very handsome. His eyes shone like dark stones on fire. His lips were red and full. His jaw was severe and masculine, and the soft, curly hair of his beard made the sisters want to reach out and touch him.

The god gently lifted one hand from each sister. They sighed; their faces flushed red. He was as warm as the sun in July. He slowly drew their hands to his mouth, and their hearts beat like tiny birds. Their bodies trembled with fear and a need so strong their legs felt weak.

"Francine." Pan gently kissed the back of Francine's hand, and her breath caught in her throat. His voice, speaking her name, was like a manifestation of his adoration. And the intimacy of his touch set her skin on fire. She could feel herself wrapped around his strong body, yet she also felt sure he was standing in front of her.

"Willa." Pan then kissed the back of Willa's hand. She couldn't look away from his dark, shimmering eyes. He said her name as if it were a promise of love and worship. She felt his hard body move against hers, yet her eyes told her he stood directly before her.

Pan's fingers caressed their palms and down their fingers, and suddenly he was many feet away, bowing to them. Their hands were glowing. A faint outline of his lips across their knuckles pulsed and faded, as if absorbed into their bodies.

"I..." said Willa. "I..."

"That was ..." said Francine. "I mean ..."

"Believe me, the pleasure was all mine." Pan smiled and he walked back toward his son. "You are his first friends on this plane. And not for lack of trying."

The sisters smiled dazedly. The Devil shook his head and grunted.

"We must now offer you a good night, or I should say, a good morning to you both."

"Wait!" said Willa, rousing from her stupor. "You never told us his name."

"Ah yes." Pan smiled and held his hand out toward the Devil in presentation. "Allow me to introduce my son, Yiós."

"Yee-ohss," repeated Willa.

"Close enough," said Pan, and he turned away.

"But wait," called Francine. "We still remember. I don't think it worked."

But Pan didn't answer, and the sisters watched the pair, god and monster — father and son — walk through a door they couldn't see and then vanish into thin air. They stared at the tall, dark pines for a long moment, quietly contemplating everything they had seen. They turned and looked at one another. Francine noticed her flashlight on the ground a few feet away and went to pick it up.

"I'm so sorry we didn't see anything, Francy." Willa grabbed her rucksack off the ground and slung it on her back.

"It's okay." Francine shrugged and then smiled. "I'm really glad you were here."

"Me too." Willa smiled.

Francine put her pack on her back, and they walked to the edge of the clearing. At the same moment, they turned and stood staring into the blackness. The fireflies danced brilliantly, and the darkness looked like velvet cloth.

"Fireflies in November," whispered Willa. "So magikal."

"It really is." Francine smiled, feeling happier than she had for a long time.

They turned and began the long trek back to the car.

"You know, I've been thinking," said Francine. "I feel rejuvenated by this hike, so maybe we come here twice a year instead of just once."

"I can't believe you said that." Willa pushed her sister in the back. "I was thinking the same thing!"

"Right?! Maybe, once in autumn and once in late winter?"

"Okay, yeah." Willa nodded. "That sounds like a great idea. How about in mid-February and then around the end of September, at the equinox?"

"Yes!" Francine agreed. "I don't know why, but I feel so good about everything."

"Me too." Willa smiled.

The sisters met the trail with a vigor seldom felt leaving the Barrens. The forest was quiet and cold, yet there was a zeal that wasn't there when they started. It was beautiful and exciting, and the sisters talked about it the entire way home.

The Secret

Susan Tulio

Leeds Point, New Jersey
1735

"What a beautiful day." A cooling breeze drifted from the coast, ruffling the wisps of hair that peeked out from underneath Eliza's white linen cap. She lifted her eyes to the clear blue sky and pulled in a deep breath.

Aaron, her betrothed, held out his hand toward her as a small smile turned up the edge of his mouth. "Come."

Eliza placed her hand in his and followed his gaze to a copse of trees that grew half a furlong from where they stood. Her feet danced along the sandy trail as Aaron's long strides pulled her down the path, out of the sunlight into the perpetual twilight that entombed the forest and shut out the day. They stood facing each other alone for the first time in their courtship.

"I have something for you," Aaron said, handing Eliza a scroll of paper he had hidden inside his linen shirt. Drawn in ink was a likeness of himself standing at the edge of a stream next to Eliza. He had captured her doe-eyed beauty and the soft curve of her lips as she picked wild orchids near the water's edge.

Eliza held the sketch against her heart. "Aaron, I will cherish this all the days we are apart."

"I love you, Liza. You are everything that matters most to me. You are my hope, my future, the dreams that live in my soul."

Eliza's heart leapt as her eyes touched on this beautiful man who spoke of his love for her as if it were a poem. She breathed in deeply as Aaron stepped closer. His masculine scent of cedar wood with a hint of smoke surrounded her. She loved how it clung to her long after he departed.

Eliza closed her eyes as he lowered his head until his lips were just a hair's breadth away. A small breathless whisper escaped as their mouths touched. It was her first kiss and a warmth spread throughout her body as she stretched up on her tiptoes.

Aaron lifted his head slowly, and Eliza swayed unsteadily on her feet. Her body trembled as she leaned in closer, wanting to feel the warmth of his broad chest through his waistcoat.

"Liza, we must return before someone remarks on our absence."

"Wait, I have something for you as well." Eliza reached inside her skirts and pulled out a lock of chestnut colored hair tied with a light blue ribbon.

She blushed as she handed it to Aaron. "'Tis nothing."

"'Tis everything, Liza." He whispered as their lips brushed softly one last time.

Leeds Point, New Jersey
Two Years Later

Eliza knelt on the damp ground repairing the henhouse, ignoring the morning dew that seeped through her skirts and dampened her stockings. Tree limbs lay scattered on the ground and she worked quickly securing the branches back into their notches. She glanced over her shoulder, checking to see if her father was about. It would be difficult to convince him that their fattest hen had been carted off by a fox, and not that other nonsense that had mushroomed throughout the Pinelands.

What had been a largely tranquil existence in a heavily forested area ringed by cedars and pines had become increasingly unsettled in recent years and even more so of late. Eliza blamed the Reverend Humphreys who perpetuated the tall tale warning his faithful flock to be on the lookout for a demonic creature. Eliza didn't believe in ghosts, hobgoblins or two-legged flying devils. It was just an unfounded story pinned on her dear friend's family whose property bordered Eliza's parent's farm.

Eliza worried her bottom lip. She wished Aaron was here. He would know how to stop the story from spreading like wildfire. He had a way with people: strong, handsome and gifted with a most pleasant nature. Eager to escape the mundane routine of rural life, he had accepted an apprenticeship with an aspiring printer and worked in Philadelphia for the past two years.

A longing so deep flooded her entire being at the thought of her betrothed, but it was quickly replaced by a heavy weight that settled in her stomach. The rumour and the pamphlet that circulated the countryside lay at the heart of her distress. No moral, God-fearing person should believe such an exaggeration about Mistress Leeds! Eliza could only shake her head at the nonsense and refused to speak of the falsehood. If only the rest of the parish were of like mind.

"You're safe now." Eliza spoke to the chickens as if they were her pets, brushing sand from her skirts. "Worry not." The sound of dead leaves being trampled broke the morning silence and her gaze shifted to the sandy path. Eliza smiled and waved. Her best friend, Hannah, ran down the gravel trail worn flat by years of travel between the two homes.

Eliza's smile vanished as Hannah stumbled into the clearing, sobbing as she flew into Eliza's outstretched arms.

"What is it? Please tell me. Is someone hurt?"

"Jonas and his father called upon us last eve," Hannah cried. "The betrothal is broken. Jonas's father will not allow the union because he fears my family is cursed."

"Poppycock," Eliza spat. "What says Jonas?" Eliza stood with her hands on her hips.

"Liza, his father would not allow him to speak to me. It all happened so fast. Mother had just put the kettle on the hearth to brew tea when Jonas's father confessed that he believed my mother conceived a child born a spawn of the devil."

"How could he be so gullible to let these lies blacken his heart and colour his judgement?"

"Liza, what will I do? My heart is without repair! I have been pledged to Jonas since a babe."

"We must find a way to prove to our neighbors that there was no such child. That your mother is without blame."

"But how?" Hannah cried.

"I will write to Aaron posthaste. He has the ear of many gentlefolk. Perhaps he can help change the tide."

Eliza forced a smile and wiped at a tear that slid down Hannah's flushed cheek.

"Liza, I fear matters will only get worse for my family. Father refuses to return home until he exposes the culprit responsible for this untruth. I am so fearful, I sleep with one eye open."

"We will write to your father also."

Eliza waited weeks for a reply to her letters. But each day there was no post rider. In the meantime, she pleaded with her own family to help extinguish the lies and undo the terrible wrong that afflicted the Leeds family. Her father promised to do his best but was caught up with the townsfolk in placing blame for the stolen chickens and slaughtered cows on some beast that invaded the area. Although he held fast that it was unlikely a creature born of the devil.

Eliza insisted, as she set out with her family for the meetinghouse, that it could have been a clever fox that broke into the hen house.

"Father, would you not agree that we have seen packs of wolves stalking our dear cows?" Eliza struggled to keep up with her father as a trickle of sweat ran down her spine, dampening the linen shift she wore under her stays. A spell of quiet, hazy weather had settled into the region as the warmth of an autumn harvest sun peeked through patches of gray clouds that looked like the wool of sheep. Eliza could manage no more than a brisk walk as the fully boned bodice restrained a sufficient breath of air from being drawn into her lungs.

"Dear Eliza, not everything can be explained so easily." Her father stopped and tugged gently on her braid.

"I disagree, Father. I insist you plead the Leeds's case and attest that there was no thirteenth child born." Eliza's voice rose louder than she had intended.

"Calm yourself, child, and I remind you to take care of your manners."

"But Father, they are prisoners in their own home. They have seen men carrying torches in the pines just beyond their yard. They are afraid to wander about lest someone lash out."

"Enough, Eliza, lower your voice. Or next Sunday you will find yourself prisoner in our own home. You are most unagreeable today. Perhaps 'tis time I write to Aaron as your days as a maid are long runneth. You should be a good wife by now." His last word was spoken like a period at the end of a sentence as he picked up his pace, leaving Eliza and the rest of her family lagging behind.

Eliza's temperament soured further as she and her family entered the great doors of the meetinghouse. She held no love for the Reverend Humphreys and his fire and brimstone sermons. They filed into their assigned pew and quietly made their greetings. The Leeds's family pew remained solemnly empty.

The reverend cleared his throat in order to gain the congregation's attention. "'Tis with a heavy heart that I must report that last eve," he paused for effect while placing a hand across his flax spun white robe, "the home of Hattie and John Applegate burned to the ground." A wave of shocked murmurs rippled through the wooden benches as the worshipers gasped amongst each other.

Reverend Humphreys pounded his fist on the pulpit to quiet the crowd. "The good Lord saved the Applegates and their three children from perishing by flame but could not shield their eyes from the horror of witnessing their home and all their belongings burned to ash." His voice escalated. "This is the work of the devil."

A roar of outrage poured from the parishioners.

Eliza turned eyes wide with fear upon her father. "Please."

Eliza's father took a deep breath and slowly stood.

"Yes, good man Somers, what have you to say?" the reverend asked.

"Reverend, 'tis not uncommon for fires to break out in the dry brush this time of year, especially with the spell of warm weather we are having."

"Do you challenge 'twas the work of the devil that has been terrorizing our countryside?" The reverend glared down from the pulpit, twisting his face into a sneer.

The pew creaked as Eliza's brother Caleb stood. He pulled his shoulders back, reaching his full height, and returned the reverend's glare. "I believe my father is justly providing another argument lest we erupt in hysteria."

"Well, I will tell you this," the reverend said, pointing his finger. "Hoofprints, like no other, were spotted in the ash that surrounded the area. This is the work of that monster." The reverend pounded his fist again and ordered the sketch to be passed around from person to person.

Eliza seethed and bit back the words that threatened to erupt, but when the sketch depicting a creature with a horse-like head, bat-like wings, claws and hooves passed to her fingers, she could no longer contain herself. She jumped from her seat, crumbling the pamphlet within her palm and tossing it at the reverend.

"There is no monster," Eliza raged. "There's no leathery-winged creature flapping around the Pine Barrens. 'Tis an utter falsehood, and you should all be ashamed of yourselves for falling prey to such nonsense."

Eliza ran from the hall. The words slung at her back mattered not. She would rather be opinionated and headstrong than easily swayed by gossip and lies. How could the townspeople turn so easily on the family that helped build the meetinghouse they worshiped in? If not for the Leeds's generosity, they would all be huddled inside a tent. Did such hate stem from jealousy? What could Titan Leeds have done to bring this wrath down upon his house?

The sketch was also a mystery. Who drew it and where did it come from? Paper was dear in these parts, but the print seemed to be of a finer quality. Eliza stared at her hand smudged with ink and then lifted it towards her nose. Her fingers smelled of fish, with a hint of ash and a touch of something woodsy and sweet. It was a unique odor, not horrible, but foreign to anything she had smelled before.

Eliza was forbidden to visit the Leeds home until the fresh round of rumours died down. Her father promised to keep watch over Hannah's family, but he could not be everywhere at once. When Eliza received word that Hannah's mother had taken to her bed, she could no longer stand idle and ignore the knot growing in the pit of her stomach. She was ten and eight now and she would do as she pleased. She packed a basket, filled with fresh baked bread, jams, vegetables and her mother's rabbit stew and set out for Hannah's home. Her feet flew in haste along the path she had traveled hundreds of times.

Six of Hannah's younger siblings played in the front yard, but it was the condition of their clothing that shocked Eliza. Although clean, their clothes were torn in places and not one of them had shoes on their feet, even though the autumn temperatures had taken hold.

The state of the household was not much better. The once beautiful large stone and brick home was in disarray. Hannah sat by the hearth working on her sewing but clutched her heart when she spotted Eliza climbing the steps of the front porch.

"Hannah, I came as soon as I heard your mother had taken ill. I brought a basket of food, but I think I should have packed two." Eliza smoothed back a strand of golden hair and stared into a pool of watery blue eyes.

"I have missed you so, dear friend," Hannah said as she wiped away a tear that slipped down her cheek.

"Father has forbidden me to visit in case the reverend's band of rebels are hiding in the woods waiting to catch the devil."

"I, too, am afraid to venture past the clearing. But soon I must. With father's almanac out of print and that horrid tale circulating, our supplies are quite low and our coffers are close to empty."

"Any word from your father?"

"A letter has been received but not with news that will reverse our misfortune. Father is still in search of the knave and lyar that has instituted this evil and refuses to depart Philadelphia until he exposes the culprit." Hannah sighed. "Father's neglection has sent my poor mother to her bed. She wants to leave this place and start over, someplace where we are less known, but father is hell-bent on his mission and cares naught of our struggle here."

"Why does your father seek the wrongdoer in Philadelphia and not at home here in the Pinelands?"

"Father insists that the sketch claiming that he and mother had a thirteenth devil child came from a press in Philadelphia."

Eliza thought back to the pamphlet she crumbled in her fist just weeks ago. She knew from Aaron there were only two printers in Philadelphia, Aaron's employer, and Andrew Bradford, who circulated the *American Weekly Mercury* newspaper. Eliza worried her bottom lip, her mind racing towards the possibility that Aaron might be apprenticing for the culprit.

"Mother fears Reverend Humphreys and his powerful influence throughout the parish. We are already treated like lepers. These lies founded our downfall and I worry we will starve come winter."

"I will not let that happen," Eliza promised.

"Please pray, Liza, that father is able to expose these falsehoods and his homecoming is anon."

Eliza returned home with a new determination. She penned a second letter to Aaron detailing the news that Hannah shared with her, warning Aaron that his employer may be without scruple. But there was still one piece missing from this query. *Why?* What did Aaron's employer or any other printer have to gain by ruining the Leeds family's good name? Guilt weighed heavily on her heart. If Eliza exposed Aaron's employer as a possible suspect for the offence, would she be endangering Aaron's future as well as her own? But how could she possibly remain close-mouthed and watch the demise of her best friend's family. Had they not already suffered enough?

"Father, you must take me to Philadelphia."

"Eliza, 'tis not a journey easy for a woman. Has Aaron not promised to come home Yuletide? You will see him then."

"'Tis more than just a visit to see Aaron. I have suspicions on who is behind the Leeds's troubles. I must speak to Aaron."

"Pray enlighten me, daughter."

Eliza explained that her theory stemmed from when she first held the pamphlet in her hands at assembly. The paper and print did not resemble the normal local literature. In addition, Hannah shared that Mr. Leeds suspected a printer out of the area as well. "What if 'tis Aaron's employer?"

Eliza's father chuckled. "That is an ambitious tale. 'Tis my duty as your father to dissuade you from such endeavors."

"And 'tis my duty to warn my betrothed that he could be in an apprenticeship with a scoundrel."

"What good say you will that do? Except mayhap cause Aaron the loss of his employment. Have you, daughter, any facts to back up your accusations?"

Eliza hesitated. "No, just my intuition that something is amiss in Philadelphia."

"Eliza, there are times when you suffer from a soaring imagination, and I must insist you redirect your energies in assisting your mother in the care of your siblings."

"Father, I beseech you not to dismiss my fears so easily."

"I can assure you, dear daughter, Titan Leeds is on the right track and will get to the bottom of these rumours soon."

"But what about Aaron? Do we just leave him in the lion's den? His reputation will be made to suffer."

"Liza, the only virtue to suffer will be your own if you try to put in question the character of a highly respected businessman, author and editor. Let sleeping dogs lie, daughter."

"Caleb, wake." Eliza shook her brother's shoulder until he stirred.

"What, can you not see that I am at rest?"

"I need your help," she whispered. "We must ride for Philadelphia. We need to leave now before the house awakens."

"But why?"

"I must see Aaron."

Caleb groaned. "Liza, this sounds like a lovesick fool's errand. Write him a letter."

"You think naught I have tried. He does not answer. Please, Caleb, I cannot be alone on the road."

"Fine," he grumbled, pulling on his breeches and gathering the rest of his clothes. "But I will not share in the blame when father learns of your folly."

"Go quickly and saddle the horses. I will follow forthwith." Eliza left him and tiptoed back to the room she shared with her sister. She donned her woolen cape and warmest mittens and placed a note on the bedside table. She worried her bottom lip as she thought over the words she had written. It was with doubt that her father would believe that her and Caleb had left before daybreak to help with the Leeds's winter chores and would return on the morrow. A sickening feeling filled Eliza's heart. Never had she lied before.

The route they traveled was scarcely a road, more of a path with trees removed. Caleb took the lead, dodging the low stumps that littered the way. Clumps of sand mixed with silt, clay and gravel flew off the horse's hooves as they pounded the soft ground. Eliza rode sidesaddle, slowing her mare a discreet distance behind Caleb lest she be covered in earth.

The horses began to tire just past midday and Caleb and Eliza stopped at the Post Road Inn to rest the animals.

"I'm dreadfully sore, Caleb," Eliza complained when she climbed into the saddle again. They had been riding for over seven hours and Caleb took pity on his sister and slowed their pace, jogging along the last of the distance. As the small port town of Gloucester loomed closer, the path turned into a smooth, hard graveled road and they were able to trot easily. The landscape changed considerably. Tall pines and cedars had been cleared from the natural surroundings, allowing for a smart row of clapboard buildings to be constructed. A backdrop of homes made of brick, logs or stone dotted the streets that twisted their way back into the forest. Men in tricorn hats and woolen coats gathered outside the Two Tun Tavern while women huddled in their woolen capes, carrying baskets filled with food items and dry goods. Eliza spotted a post rider outside the tavern and wondered if her letters were somehow trapped inside his saddle bag as she and Caleb made their way to the river's edge.

Eliza used half of her shillings to secure travel on a barge-like boat capable of carrying passengers across the Delaware River. It was the most frightening experience she had faced thus far. Not only did she have to balance her weight upon the tree limbs roped together to form a deck, but she also had to steady her sweet mare who was having difficulty finding her sea legs.

"I have never been so happy as to set foot on land," Eliza said, steadying herself against the wharf's rail. The West Shipyard port was crowded and noisy as dock workers loaded and unloaded the barges and ushered passengers to the ferry.

"You look a little green around the gills, dear sister." Caleb laughed. "Aaron will certainly appreciate your efforts."

"'Tis more than just a visit to see Aaron. I must help Hannah right the wrong that has been inflicted upon her family."

"I am actually quite pleased that her betrothal has been broken with Jonas. She could do better than that towheaded simpleton."

"Why would you say such a thing?" Eliza asked as they left the waterfront and led their horses up a stone passageway that connected them to Front Street.

"Eliza, what idiot would believe that Mistress Leeds had another baby? 'Tis hard to hide such a thing. We are a small parish, with little to no secrets. If Jonas truly loved Hannah, then he would not have let the betrothal be broken."

"You make a strong argument. But still her heart is broken."

"Not for long."

"What do you mean?"

"Upon our return home, I should like to call on Hannah."

"To court her?" Eliza stopped mid-stride.

"Yes, why are you so surprised, Liza? Am I not worthy?"

"Of course, you are worthy. I just never looked upon you in that manner." Eliza's eyes swept over her brother. She admitted his features were smart with a noble nose, strong chin and the same soft brown eyes as her own. Caleb and Hannah would make a handsome couple.

"I will be turning two and twenty soon. I have made a name for myself as a saddler and 'tis time I took a wife."

Caleb and Eliza reached Front Street and found the area teeming with activity. Men shouted at each other trying to be heard over the noise of horses' hooves striking the ground. Coachmen yelled at anyone in their way as their carriages barreled past. It was a shocking change from the Pine Barrens. Eliza covered her nose with her mitten, as the rancid smell of feces and rotting food littered the streets. Her stomach heaved as she turned wide eyes to Caleb.

"Don't look upon me, dear sister. I brought us thus far, 'tis your turn."

Eliza worried her lip and headed for the Penny Pot Tavern. "Caleb, go inside and ask them where we may find the print shop."

Caleb was given directions to High Street. "We are to look for the milliner and the apothecary on the corner and then we should spot the printers."

Caleb took the lead and headed down Second Street, finally stopping at a brick row of Georgian-style shops. "Look, I think we have found the printer."

He helped Eliza from her mount, tied their horses to a hitching rail and entered the shop. A small bell chimed as they opened the door but served no purpose, as the deafening clatter of a printing press shook the walls.

Eliza hesitated within the threshold and for the second time this day buried her nose within her mitten. The sharp smell of oil and charred ash filled the room, but there was also an underlying scent of sweetness, like incense.

"By God, this place stinks of burnt cod." Caleb made a face as he took a step forward and pointed to a corner of the room where a drawing table was placed by a large paned window to catch the fading light.

Aaron was seated on a wooden stool, head bent low, concentrating on his work. His eyes widened in surprise as he caught sight of Eliza and her brother. He jumped from the stool, knocking it backwards, and rushed to gather her into his arms.

The brief embrace ended too quickly for Eliza as Aaron pulled away. His eyes darted above her head to Caleb as a look of alarm crossed his features.

"What brings you here?" Aaron said, but barely a sound could be heard. He tossed his quill onto his desk, closed up the pewter inkpot and pulled the cotton from his ears. He motioned for Caleb and Eliza to follow him and led them down a narrow staircase to the basement.

Pine planks covered the floor of a large open room made of brick. On the far wall sat a stone hearth big enough to house a cow. Four narrow beds covered in wool blankets were spaced evenly throughout, with a trunk at the base for storage and a small table holding a bedside lamp. The basement was dark except for a few narrow windows cut just below the ceiling. Aaron quickly lit a candle. He drew Eliza into his arms again, holding her tightly until Caleb coughed uncomfortably.

"Eliza, what in the world brings you here? Is it my family?" Aaron asked. He released her from his embrace but held fast to her hand.

"Your family fares well. But I just had to see you. You have not answered my letters."

"I am sorry, Liza. I have been heavily laden with work and had naught a chance to reply."

"Something is very amiss back home," Eliza said. "Foul rumours circulate our countryside. A drawing of a leather-winged devil with the face of a goat and hooves of a horse is said to be the thirteenth child of the Leeds family. They blame the creature with the theft of our chickens and the slaughter of our cows."

"Slow down, Liza. This tale you retell is too unlikely to be believed."

"I agree, Aaron, but the Reverend Humphreys has convinced all who live in the area 'tis true."

Aaron sat down heavily on his bed and raked a hand through his hair.

Eliza noticed that he looked pale. A bead of sweat broke out on his brow, and she sat down next to him and took his hand into hers. "You look unwell."

"'Tis nothing. It is just that this news has me most distressed. Is there more?"

"Aye, there is more," Caleb added. "Jonas broke off his betrothal with Hannah and the Applegate's farm burned to the ground."

"These events are unsettling," Aaron said in a voice barely more than a whisper as he lowered his gaze to the floor. "But I do not fathom how I can be of help."

Eliza inhaled deeply. "Hannah's father suspects the printing of the sketch was done in Philadelphia. I fear your employer could be the guilty party."

Aaron scrubbed a hand down his face. "Hush, Liza. Such talk will jeopardize my position."

"That is what father said but I thought it prudent that you should know. Promise me you will take care and not fall victim to a scoundrel."

"You have my word, Liza. But I must stress that the proprietor of this print shop is most honorable and holds the respect of many. Mayhaps it is all a misunderstanding."

"I think not, Aaron. Our community hunts the creature with torch and pitchfork. The Leeds' cannot leave their home without worry for their own safety. This is no folly."

"It sounds most grave, but the hour grows late. Have you lodging for the night?" Aaron asked.

"No, but I still have one more visit. Have you knowledge where Hannah's father resides?"

"Come, I will escort you."

Eliza was exhausted by the time they arrived at the Quince Street Inn. The red brick row sat on a quiet tree-lined alley barely wide enough for a horse and cart. It appeared more upscale than the Penny Pot Tavern she and Caleb encountered earlier. Aaron found a table in the corner, and Eliza realized that she had not eaten since early morn' when they broke their fast by the stream. Her stomach rumbled as she sank into the wooden chair.

"Are you sure Hannah's father rents lodging here?" Eliza asked Aaron as she glanced around the room at the well-dressed patrons. She felt very provincial in her woolen cape and muddied skirts. Eliza smoothed a few wisps of hair that escaped from her cap as men in lace ruffles, blue coats, and knee breeches the color of buff dined with women dressed in silks with filmy wraps draped around their shoulders.

Eliza fumed. Hannah's family was practically starving while her father lived in lavish accommodations. They had just finished their dinner of pork, potatoes and rice when Titan lumbered through the door. He carried three large, rather hefty looking books and struggled to keep them sliding from under his arm. Aaron waved him over and a smile lit up Titan's face when he saw the trio.

Titan placed the books he was carrying on the table and removed his tricorn. "Good evening, Aaron, Eliza, Caleb. How does your family?"

"Our family fares well," Eliza replied, "'tis your own that I am here to speak of."

"Pray, tell me, is something amiss?"

"You must return to Leeds Point. The rumours have escalated, and your family is in fear of leaving their home. The food stores are low, and Jonas has broken his betrothal to Hannah." Eliza was out of breath by the time she finished.

"Alas, I cannot leave right now. I have been studying with John Bartram. He has many theories on how to make our crops prosper in the sandy, acidic soil of the Pinelands."

"The success of our crops is important, I agree," Eliza said, "but according to your last letter, Hannah entrusted that you were tracking down the person responsible for the rumours."

"Aye, at first, but now I have found more rewarding work."

"But what about your family? Mistress Leeds has taken to her bed." Eliza's voice shook. She could not believe the words that fell upon her ears. For a split second her breathing was suspended, and then she fired off one last sentence. "Have you no conscience or sense of responsibility?"

Aaron's eyebrows lifted while Caleb smiled and shook his head.

Titan stood. "I must take my leave. Do not overtax yourself, Eliza. Although the tale of the devil percolates and ferments throughout our community, 'twill lose its credibility before long when my rival is satisfied that I am no longer a threat to his livelihood." Titan reached into his waistcoat and removed a purse heavy with coin. "I have found much to be grateful for in the year I have been in Philadelphia. Real property opportunities abound for an ambitious man like myself. In fact, I am the proprietor of this establishment. I will leave word with the innkeeper that you will require lodging for the night. Take this to my sweet Hannah. It should provide for all the family needs until my homecoming."

Eliza ignored the pouch placed on the table and frowned at Mr. Leeds. Disappointment burned the back of her throat. 'Twas a fool's errand, indeed!

"Hush, Duchess!" Eliza hissed at her family's beloved terrier who weaved its way in and out of her mare's hooves as she entered the clearing. "Stop your barking." But it was already too late. The front door opened and standing upon the threshold was her father with his legs planted wide and his arms folded across his chest.

"Look who awaits us," Caleb said as he reined in and pulled his mount alongside Eliza's mare. "Have you a plan?"

"'Tis of no use now." Eliza had hoped her father would be elsewhere, affording her the opportunity to slip into the house unseen and change out of her muddied traveling clothes. "The truth, I suppose. Father has little tolerance for lyars."

Eliza's father descended the steps and walked slowly to where Eliza dismounted from her horse. "I would have hoped my two eldest would have brains larger than a chicken's inside their heads." He growled.

A muscle twitched on the side of her father's cheek and Eliza swallowed the lump in the back of her throat.

"You could have gotten hurt or killed. All for the folly of seeing your betrothed."

"I was trying to help Hannah," Eliza shot back, unable to hide the frustration from her voice. She dropped her eyes to the ground, not wanting her father to see the tears that burned the back of her eyelids. Did he not understand the pain it caused Eliza to watch Hannah's family ripped to shreds?

"Leave the Leeds's business to themselves, daughter. No good will come with your meddling in other's affairs."

"Someone must help. Mr. Leeds brushed off my concerns and handed me a purse filled with coin to appease his family. He seems content to live the life of a city-dweller and leave them alone to suffer."

"You will stay clear of this business, Eliza. I forbid you to continue on this path."

Eliza bit back the retort that almost flew from her lips. The word forbid quickened the blood through her veins and she could feel the heat flushing through her body.

Father took the reins of their horses. "No mounts for either of you until the first of the new year. Caleb, starting on the morrow, along with your normal chores you will now take over the chores of the young'uns at the Leeds's home. You see, daughter, I am not without heart. As for you, Liza, you will muck the stable each morn' until I tell you not to."

Caleb turned away. But not before Eliza caught the slow smile that built across his face. This was no punishment at all for her brother, for now he would be rewarded with Hannah's presence each morn.

Eliza folded her arms across her chest and drew in a deep breath. She remained silent until her father retreated, slamming the door as he entered the house. It was unfair that he insisted she just let it go when Eliza felt she was so close to unearthing the culprit.

Eliza almost dropped the pine garland that was draped across her arm as a tremor shook the ladder she stood upon. Her heartbeat quickened as she quickly attached the last of the boughs to the outside of the house with a wide red ribbon. The ladder wobbled again and Eliza climbed down just in time to see Aaron's horse and cart pulling into the yard that surrounded her home.

"Aaron, you are home at last," she said, running into his outstretched arms. "Oh, how I have missed you." She turned her face up to his, craving the warmth of his lips.

Aaron deepened the kiss, locking Eliza in his embrace as he molded his body into hers causing a warmth to flow straight to the core of her being.

"And I you, sweet Liza," he said, finally pulling away.

They made the Christmastime rounds of church socials and visits to neighbors' homes, gifting each with decorated yuletide logs and sweets Aaron brought from Philadelphia. Caleb and Hannah were always in tow, and Eliza thought she had never seen her brother and best friend so merry of soul. The purse of money that Eliza delivered to Hannah helped to make the winter months easier, and her family was no longer in danger of starving. The two couples rang in the new year with a glass of Madeira and Aaron made a promise to Eliza that they would marry come summer.

"Must you leave on the morrow?" Eliza asked.

"'Tis time, Liza. I have been away from my duties for over a week."

Caleb cleared his throat, ending the brief pang of melancholy, and announced that he would ride soon for Philadelphia to ask Hannah's father for her hand in marriage. But as the second month of the new year approached, there was no longer the need. Grim news arrived in Leeds Point. A letter, penned by Mrs. Beatrice Logan, a Quaker widow, wrote that Titan fell victim to the epidemic of smallpox that had invaded Philadelphia and had died under her care. Upon her husband's demise, Mother Leeds granted permission for Caleb and Hannah to marry under one stipulation, that Caleb move them down the coast south of Leeds Point.

Word spread throughout the Pinelands of Titan Leeds' passing. The cold temperatures kept most of the townsfolk sheltered in their homes and a calm settled over the area. Caleb and Hannah requested permission from Reverend Humphreys to forgo the normal mourning period and asked if their banns could be announced. A date for their nuptials was set three weeks hence. The eve before the wedding was to take place, a wet snow blanketed the ground covering the roofs in white. Tree limbs, heavily laden in ice, bowed gracefully along the drive as guests arrived in horse drawn sleighs.

In front of a glowing fire in the Leeds' parlor, Caleb and Hannah married on the twenty-eighth day of February 1738. Outside, flurries swirled as the sun reflected off the white landscape, making the area sparkle as if adorned in thousands of crystals.

"I will miss you, dear friend," Eliza said, embracing Hannah.

"And I you, dear Liza. You have been a true friend and a great champion in my times of distress. I wish I could be as brave as you."

"I wish you were not departing come spring."

"We must. We need a new beginning. Where Mother can rest easy. And 'tis not so far. Just a half day's journey to Somers Point. Your dear uncle was most kind in gifting us with a track of land for our very own. We will build a fine house large enough for mother and my siblings with the funds collected from the sale of my father's holdings in Philadelphia."

Eliza brushed a tear away and half-smiled at Hannah. She would not spoil her dear sister-in-law's day. The thought of not being able to walk the path that connected their two homes felt like a stab to her heart. They had been fast friends since toddlers even though they had plenty of siblings to keep them company. There was a kindness about Hannah that allowed Eliza to open her heart and share her hopes, dreams and deepest secrets. Hannah would forever remain her dearest confidante no matter the distance to her new home in Somers Point.

Eliza and Aaron's wedding took place the first Saturday in June. Eliza stood in the parlor as her mother fussed with her skirts. She wore a gown of blue with a ruffled neckline and a ripple of lace around the elbow-length sleeves. A stomacher of embroidered pink flowers and wispy green leaves adorned the front of her dress and matched the bouquet she carried. Her brown hair was braided elegantly under a white cap and pulled to the side of her neck trailing over her shoulder. Butterflies fluttered in her stomach but not from nerves. She truly loved Aaron and was excited to share the intimacy of marriage with him. They had managed little more than a few kisses thus far, but once Aaron had coerced her lips to part and let his tongue tangle with hers. Eliza's breath quickened and a tingling sensation spread straight to her most private place. When she leaned her body into his she could feel his maleness harden.

"'Tis time to begin," Reverend Humphreys announced, pulling Eliza into the present.

Eliza forced a smile. Her wedding nuptials were all to her liking except for the fact that the Reverend Humphreys was in attendance.

The reverend led Eliza and Aaron out the porch door, down the wooden steps of her home, and to the meadow behind her house. Eliza's parents followed next, and then Hannah and Caleb as bridesmaid and bridesman.

The reverend ended the procession and stood before her and Aaron holding the Book of Common Prayer. "Wilt thou have this Man as thy wedded Husband, to live together after God's Ordinance, in the holy Estate of Matrimony? Wilt thou obey him, serve him, love, honour and keep him in sickness and in health, and forsaking all others, keep thee only unto him, so long as ye both shall live?" Reverend Humphreys asked.

"I do," Eliza replied, gazing deeply into Aaron's eyes.

Aaron took Eliza's hand in his and repeated the

words the Reverend Humphreys spoke. "With this ring I thee wed," he said, slipping a simple band of metal on her finger. "With thy body I thee worship, and with all my worldly goods I thee endow."

A cheer of joy erupted from the wedding guests as the reverend pronounced them man and wife and Aaron tipped Eliza's chin up for the briefest of kisses. Eliza felt herself blush straight through to her hairline as the cheers grew louder. The reverend cleared his throat and motioned for Eliza and Aaron to follow him to a table that held the parish registry. He handed the inkpot to Eliza and the quill to Aaron and traced his finger down the page to where he needed their signatures. Eliza lifted the lid on the brass inkpot and wrinkled her nose at the odor.

"Reverend, your inkpot has a very distinct smell," Eliza said.

"That it does. 'Twas a gift imported all the way from Holland."

Eliza's eyebrows lifted. "Indeed." She was about to question him deeper, but Aaron pulled her away, impatient to join the party. There was much food and drink and toasting along with games and plenty of dancing. Eliza visited with Hannah who confided to her that she and Caleb would be expecting a child come Yuletide. Eliza hugged her close and then twirled her around and onto the makeshift platform as they joined the other dancers in a simple country reel.

Reverend Humphreys was one of the last wedding guests to depart. Eliza turned up her nose as she watched him stagger amongst the partygoers. He seemed to be laughing at something Aaron's employer had said as he shook his hand and slapped him on the back. Eliza watched thoughtfully. She knew the two were guilty of the malicious slander. It made sense. The acrid smelling ink was the same odor as the print shop in Philadelphia, and it tied the two men together.

Eliza suspected Aaron's employer convinced the reverend to distribute the drawing and spread the lie about the Leeds and put Titan Leeds's prosperous almanac out of business. Eliza's eyes narrowed on the pair and she was just about to confront them with her suspicions when Aaron slipped an arm around her waist and pulled her close.

"You have the look of someone who is vexed, sweet bride. What bothers you?"

"'Twas them." Eliza directed her gaze across the yard to where the reverend stood. "They are at the beginnings of the tale that consumed our community. I know it, and wish to have a word with them."

"I see two men well into their cups and nothing more," Aaron said.

His eyes reflected the joy of the day and Eliza swallowed her argument, deciding not to spoil their celebration. She needed no more evidence. The ink that stained her hands from the pamphlet she balled into her fist months ago had the same distinct smell of the print shop Aaron worked at in Philadelphia, and the reverend's inkpot. The ink Eliza used to pen her own letters held no such odor. In truth, the inkpot on her father's desk held the faintest scent of urine.

However, 'twas her wedding day, a day for laughter and dancing. For now, she would dance with her husband before they retired to their marriage bed—although she couldn't help but keep a sharp eye on the Reverend Humphreys and Aaron's employer, Mr. Benjamin Franklin.

Philadelphia – 2020

Wells Davis, project manager for the Historical Society of Pennsylvania, stood outside the narrow brick row at Second and Market Streets. He frowned at the sign that hung from the eighteenth-century paneled door announcing that the museum was closed for repairs. It had been two weeks already and he worried over the length of time it would take to fortify the basement infrastructure.

Wells had handpicked the two restoration preservationists for their expertise at repairing foundations and walls that were once built of brick and stone but today resembled nothing more than crumbly pebbles. He visited often, checking their progress and overseeing any new developments that might be hindering the process.

He adjusted his eyes to the dimly lit space, surprised to find the two workers prying paneling off a far wall one board at a time.

"Jake, what's going on? Why aren't you working on the foundation?" Wells asked, not really wanting to hear the answer.

Amy, Jake's co-worker, climbed down from the ladder she had been using to help her reach the upper planks.

"Hey, Mr. Davis, this morning I found a puddle of water on the floor. As soon as we get this rotted wood off, we'll be able to see where it's coming from."

"These old buildings, fix one thing and ten more problems appear," Jake said as he drove a flat bar beneath a plank, pulling it from the wall.

"Mind if I stick around? I'd like to see how big of a headache we have on our hands." Wells couldn't hide the note of dread from his voice as he ducked out of the way of a four-foot piece of paneling.

Soon a hearth, flush with the wall, wide and deep, was revealed. The scorched red brick interior housed multiple areas for cooking and baking and still looked to have some of the original pot hooks and iron bars running the length of the fireplace. A wall of crumbling stone rose above the briefest semblance of a mantel and continued to the ceiling. The leak was coming from the chimney.

"Hey, check this out," Jake said, removing a loose rock whose mortar was missing.

Wells and Amy stood just behind Jake as he slipped on a pair of white cotton gloves. Hidden behind the loose stone was a dry, brittle piece of rag paper, faded to a soft latte color. Jake lifted a corner and unfolded it to reveal a lock of brown hair tied with a light blue ribbon, a drawing and a note written in very flowy script.

My Dearest Eliza, *Philadelphia 12 Nov 1737*

What joy it brought to my heart to see the splendour of your face. And yet I feel I have marred our reunion with silence and half-truths. It has never been my wish to keep secrets from you, but unknowingly I have caused harm to those we love. I thought nothing to discourage the request from my employer to produce a rendering of a beast with grotesque features. Nor did I know that the drawing was to be the catalyst for the demise of the Leeds's livelihood. I look upon myself with shame and horror at the destruction I have created by simple pen and paper. I fear you will no longer look upon me with love but with judgement. What I have done is without scruple but I innocently knew little of the rivalry between Titan Leeds and Mr. Franklin. I pray that God will give me the courage to send this letter to you thus placing our future in your beloved hands.

A

"Look at the date on the note. I'm amazed it's still intact." Jake cradled the document in the palm of his hands like it was a baby hamster.

"What's the drawing of?" Amy asked. "It looks like an emaciated flying horse."

"That's the Jersey Devil," Jake answered.

"Like the hockey team?"

Wells laughed. "Yes and no. The hockey team borrowed the name from the Jersey Devil, but that's about it. The real Jersey Devil has a horse-like head, bat-like wings, claws and hooves."

"I never heard of it." Amy shrugged. "So, what's the note about?"

"Maybe I can fill in some of the blanks," Wells began. "As you know, this is the building where the *Poor Richard's Almanac* was printed by Ben Franklin. The basement was used as a sort of dormitory for the young men who worked for him. In 1735, a very real rivalry existed between Titan Leeds and Ben Franklin. Apparently, ole Ben felt there was only enough business for one almanac. A rumor accompanied by a pamphlet spread throughout the Pine Barrens stating that Titan Leeds's wife had a thirteenth child and that somehow it had become cursed and was born a devil."

"So, you think this *A* guy was the artist behind the drawing?" Jake asked.

"Sounds like it. And if this letter and drawing are authentic, they will finally prove that the legend of the Jersey Devil was all a hoax schemed up by our dear founding father who had quite the sense of humor." Wells pulled a large, airtight plastic bag from Jake's toolbox and held it open while Jake slipped the drawing and letter inside. "I'll hand deliver this to the lab. Since Franklin imported an exclusive blend of Dutch Ink from Holland, it should be a pretty simple test."

"Do you think Eliza ever learned the truth?" Amy

asked, a frown wrinkling her brow as she rolled the lock of hair between her fingers before dropping it into the bag. "Or did we just uncover a three-hundred-year-old secret?"

"My guess is that she probably found out when they were old and gray," Jake said.

"Nah," Amy shook her head, offering a difference of opinion. "I bet he told her in person instead of sending the letter. Plus, I think she forgave him for the part he was forced to play."

Wells listened to the exchange between Jake and Amy with interest. It wouldn't hurt to do some investigating on his own and find out the names of the illustrators who worked for Franklin at the time. If he could identify *A*, then he could check to see if a marriage was ever registered. Luckily, church vital records often dated back into the 1700s.

Two weeks later Wells had his results.

"Hey, you two, mind taking a short walk. I've something interesting to show you."

Wells led Jake and Amy to the Christ Church burial ground. He paid the admission, bypassed the crowd gathered around Franklin's grave, and headed to the southeast corner of the cemetery. Against a red brick wall stood the Harwood Family Monument.

"You found her," Amy said, her eyes lighting up as a smile broke out across her face.

"I did. Turns out, Eliza Somers married Aaron Harwood on June 7, 1738. Just about eight months after the letter was written. They moved to Philadelphia and purchased a home at 229 Mulberry Street where they raised four children: Jacob, Joshua, Clinton and Rachel. Sadly, her oldest and youngest sons were lost to the American Revolution while fighting for General George Washington when the British took Philadelphia. It was noted that Rachel Harwood, alongside her mother, worked tirelessly filling cardboard tubes with gun powder. It was even recorded that they hand delivered the ammunition by horse straight to Fort Mifflin."

"Wow, that's pretty amazing," Amy said.

A bell tolled in the distance as all three silently paid tribute focusing on the epitaph inscribed under Eliza's name: A Heroine to the American Revolution.

About the Authors

Author, artist, and musician, ***LCW Allingham*** has stories published in several anthologies and in the ancient texts of things foretold.

H. A. Callum has traveled far and wide but set wanderlust aside and landed right back where he started in the Philadelphia suburbs. When not wielding the pen, he's chasing unicorns with his daughters because every writer knows the imagination exceeds speculation. Mr. Callum's poetry and fiction have appeared in local and national literary journals. His debut literary novel, "Whispers in the Alders," was published by Brown Posey Press in 2018.

River Eno is vegan, a studying herbalist, and the author of the Urban Fantasy novels, "The Anastasia Evolution Series." Her corporeal shell resides on the East Coast in this reality while her brain travels to alternate realities daily.

Melissa D. Sullivan is a writer, parent and semi-professional Tina Fey fangirl. Melissa's writing has appeared in Hippocampus Magazine, Nightingale & Sparrow, Sum Journal and elsewhere, and her short story, "Dear Jacqueline," was nominated for a 2019 Pushcart Prize. She can often be found in the suburbs of Philadelphia, eating Taco Bell and plotting out her next strong female lead.

Susan Tulio enjoys writing romances for their optimistic outlook and charm unique to any other form of fiction. She lives near Philadelphia, Pennsylvania and is currently at work on a new novel.

Made in the USA
Monee, IL
11 March 2020

22911230R00105